Heaven looks A LOT LIKE the mall

a novel by Wendy Mass

Little, Brown and Company
Books for Young Readers
New York   Boston

Also by Wendy Mass:

A Mango-Shaped Space
Leap Day
Jeremy Fink and the Meaning of Life
Every Soul a Star

Little, Brown and Company

Hachette Book Group
237 Park Avenue, New York, NY 10017
Visit our Web site at www.lb-teens.com

Little, Brown and Company is a division of Hachette Book Group, Inc.
The Little, Brown name and logo are trademarks of Hachette Book Group, Inc.

First Paperback Edition: November 2008
First published in hardcover in 2007 by Little, Brown and Company

Library of Congress Cataloging-in-Publication Data

Mass, Wendy 1967-
  Heaven looks a lot like a mall/by Wendy Mass. — 1st ed.
      p. cm.
  Summary: When high school junior Tessa Reynolds falls into a coma after getting hit in the head during gym class, she experiences heaven as the mall where her parents work, and she revisits key events from her life, causing her to reevaluate herself and how she wants to live.
  ISBN: 978-0-316-05851-3 (hardcover) / 978-0-316-05850-6 (paperback)
  (1. Shopping malls — Fiction. 2. Schools — Fiction. 3. Coma — Fiction. 4. Self-realization — Fiction.) I. Title.
PZ7.M42355He 2007
(Fic)—dc22   2007012333

HC: 10 9 8 7 6 5 4 3 2
PB: 10 9 8 7 6 5 4 3 2 1

RRD-C

Printed in the United States of America

This book is dedicated to all the teenagers who shared tales of their childhood misadventures, and who reminded me that sometimes being bad feels good, and sometimes being bad feels bad, and you never can tell beforehand.

I also want to thank Judy Blume, who read the first paragraph a long time ago, and made me promise to use it in a book some day. So if you don't like it, blame her.
(But seriously, don't.)

And to Randi Goldberg, who after twenty-five years is still the person I enjoy going to the mall with the most.

it's a mall world

Dodgeball

I.

For fifty cents and a Gobstopper
I lifted my shirt for the neighborhood boys.
My older brother Matt caught us
and chased the boys with a
Wiffle bat.
Word got around, and at nine years old
I became the girl
other girls' moms
didn't want them to play with.

For some reason,
this is the memory in my head

as the fluorescent orange dodgeball
hurtles toward me at something like
the speed of light, but in slow motion
at the same time.

In my high school there are jocks,
preps, cheerleaders, teachers' pets,
hicks, stoners, slackers, dorks, cool kids,
band/choir/chorus/drama geeks,
regular geeks, nerds, populars, burnouts,
freaks, punks, intellectuals, scene kids,
emo kids, goths, loners, losers, wankstas,
sluts, haters, skaters, speds, straight-edgers,
floaters, and drifters. And yet *I'm* the one
someone has chosen as a dodgeball target.

I stare at the orange ball, unable to move,
and I wonder, which came first,
the color orange, or the fruit?
And why is an orange the only fruit
that has to share its name with its color?
A banana isn't called *yellow*.
It's not fair.
If I were an orange, I would complain.

If I were an orange, I wouldn't be
standing here in dorky gym shorts,
which are too tight in the thighs/butt
(and not in a good way.)
I wouldn't have to take gym class at all,

where everyone can see that I missed
shaving that stripe of hair
on the back of my legs.

I don't know who fired this ball,
but they should get a major league contract
instead of applying to college.

II.

Speaking of college,
why are my parents making me
write my college application essay
when there's still two weeks of junior year left?

And why does the essay question have to be so hard?
Who are you?
They have the nerve to ask me this,
and then tell me I can attach extra paper,
if I need it.

Who *am* I?
I have no idea.
I mean, I don't even have the slightest,
vaguest clue. Well, I know the basics.
My name, shoe size, bra size,
favorite color, and what I ate for breakfast,
but I don't think that's what they mean.

I bet Amanda Jentis knows who she is —
the most popular girl in school
with a thousand friends on her MySpace.
Once, she smiled at me in the hall
and said, "Cute shirt." I think she meant it too,
because her friend Allie didn't laugh
and ask, "Were you *serious*?"
like she did when Amanda told some freshman
that she liked his haircut.

And to top it all off,
an old Ashlee Simpson song
keeps going through my head
as if I haven't sworn off boys.

Hey, how long till you're leaving me alone,
Don't you got somewhere to go?
I didn't steal your boyfriend.
These gym shorts are giving me a wedgie.
Should I fix them? I probably don't have time,
on account of the ball.

Out of the corner of my eye
I see Andy Beckerman —
who I once had a sort of date with —
staring at my butt.
Can he see the wedgie?
Or is he just thinking I have a big butt?

The time to duck, or move out of the way,
is rapidly approaching. Any normal person
would duck. It's, like, a natural human reaction.
Ball-whizzing-toward-head equals DUCK.
Why aren't I ducking?

III.

I could say, in my defense,
the dodgeball is made of rubber.
How much damage
could a rubber ball do?
I am sixteen.
My head is hard.

And who thinks aiming balls
at someone's head is a healthy pursuit
for teenagers hyped up on caffeine?
Apparently dodgeball is banned
in most schools now,
but our principal does not believe
in banning. Our school library
takes pride in its collection of books
that have been banned
elsewhere.

I watch the ball get closer
and closer as my teammates

move farther
and farther away from me.

I watch, mesmerized, as it smacks
the blond girl – not a natural blond,
but you wouldn't know it
unless you looked really hard at her roots –
squarely on the left side of her head.
I watch her neck bend back
at a really weird angle.
I watch as she falls,

not crumpling gracefully
like in the movies,
but slamming hard
onto the shiny gym floor.

I wonder if some people are thinking
this is the most exciting thing to happen
in gym since Claire Franklin and Billy Sams
were caught doing it behind the bleachers.

IV.

I watch as the others run toward her,
some screaming and others smiling,
and I don't blame the ones
who are smiling. I know that sometimes
when presented with a real-life shock

you don't know how to handle it,
so you smile like when you're watching
a movie and it's supposed to be entertaining,
but you're like, *this is just violent,*
why is this supposed to be entertaining?
but then you smile anyway
because the actor or actress is really cute
and says something sarcastic and you try
not to look at the body while you wait
for the next scene.

I watch the gym teacher yell "Stand back"
and for someone to get the school nurse.
The janitor arrives
I guess to wipe up the blood.

I know the girl on the floor, the one
with her neck bent all weird,
I know the girl is me.
But I'm too busy soaring
toward Heaven to care.

And the thing that is most surprising,
the thing you might not know,
is that in the right light,
Heaven looks a lot like the mall.

Information Booth

I.

When I land – well, not so much land,
exactly, but stop soaring – I find myself
standing in front of the Information Booth.

It is not just any information booth,
at any mall, in any town.
I am at MY OWN MALL,
in my own town.
There may be thirty thousand
malls in America,
but I would recognize mine anywhere.
The sprawling brick and glass

and linoleum structure
filled with everything
anyone would ever need.

But how did I get here?
Did I drive? Is Matt home
from college and he drove me?
Did my parents bring me
to work with them?

The last thing I remember
I was sprawled, spread-eagle
on the gym floor,
which is not a very ladylike position,
and my mother would have been horrified
if she knew, because appearances
are very, very important
to her.

Okay. I might not be
the smartest pair of jeans on the rack,
but I'm pretty sure I know
what's going on.
I just never believed
in an afterlife before.

And to be honest, I always thought
mine would come in shades of red
and heat. I never thought I would be
lucky enough to wind up here,

where I feel more at home
than my real home.
Both of my parents work here,
and over the years I've spent
more time here than anywhere
except for school.

I know the mall like the back of my hand,
although when you think about it,
that expression is really dumb,
because if someone showed me
the back of my hand, and then the back
of someone else's hand,
could I truly tell the difference?
And why does the blood in my veins
look blue, when the gym floor proves
it is red?

I love the mall. I love the smooth, shiny floors,
the marble and chrome that make you feel
like an honored guest. I love the skylights
that fill the open spaces with shafts of light,
the escalators that lead you up to the bounty
of riches on the top floor, Gucci and Fendi,
Godiva and Betsey Johnson, Tiffany and Lucky –
all the places out of my reach. I love the flowering
plants and gurgling fountains that make you think
it's summer in the middle of March.

I know the tricks stores use to keep customers
inside, like the absence of windows so you won't know
how late it is, the music they play to keep you
energized, the lighting in the dressing rooms
that makes you look tanner, the way the mirrors
are slightly tilted forward to make you look thinner.
I know where the security cameras are hidden –
behind the trees, under the posters,
inside the light fixtures.

I know they bunch together all the teenage stores
like Aeropostale, PacSun, A&F, American Eagle,
Hollister, Rampage, Hot Topic, Spencer's, and Wet Seal
so the rest of the mall doesn't have to deal with us,
and the security guys won't have to follow us
as far. They don't follow me at all
because I'm a mall brat, which is like an army brat,
except your parents work here instead of in the army,
and it's an unspoken agreement
that we would never steal from ourselves
except sometimes we do.

I have spent so much
of my life in this mall,
I suppose it is only fitting that I spend
eternity here as well.

II.

But where is the pearly gate?
Where are the angels and harps?
(Not that I really like harps. I mean,
honestly, who does? But still,
what is Heaven without harps?)

At least being dead
I won't ever have to write
that stupid college essay.

I guess now I'll never find out
who I am. Or was. Or would have been.
Although let's face it, my future
wasn't so bright that I'd have to wear shades.

I bet a lot of kids
would be royally ticked off
if they died during dodgeball.
They would feel betrayed
and maybe angry or sad.
But I have perfected the art
of not feeling
anything at all.

In a way, this whole dying thing
takes a lot of the pressure off.
It's just too hard trying not to cross

all those fine lines that everyone is aware of,
even though they don't talk about them:

Be honest, but don't hurt anyone's feelings
be independent, but not a loner
be smart, but not a nerd
be sexy, but not a slut
be skinny, but don't barf up your burger
be funny, but not to hide some other deficiency.
How the heck is a girl
supposed to "be" anything?

I look around at the shops on either side
of the Information Booth.
I bet I could shop for free!

I could ask Old Bev because she's been here
since the mall opened in the eighties,
and she's always in her little chair
giving someone directions to Pottery Barn
or the AMC theaters or Burger King, and she would
   know
if the dead people can shop for free.

Some people say she looks
like she was put together with spare parts,
and maybe she does, but she's always been
really sweet to me.

But Bev is not manning the booth.
In fact, I see no one else in the entire mall.
Which is weird, since gym class is smack
in the middle of the day.

I look up through the big skylight. No sky,
no clouds, no stars. Only blackness.
I ring the bell on the counter anyway.
The echo bounces off empty walls
and cavernous spaces. Then I notice
a note taped to the counter:

Tessa Reynolds (that's me!),
Welcome to The Mall of Heaven.
Hang on for the ride of your life.
— The Mall Manager

It slowly dawns on me
(nothing dawns on me quickly,
as proven by my mediocre SAT scores)
that someone's gone to a lot of effort
to make me comfortable.
I wonder if to my father, Heaven
looks a lot like a bowling alley.

Hot Dog-on-a-Stick

I.

I plop down next to the Info Booth,
on the white plastic bench
made possible by a generous donation
from the Elks Club.
I wait. I wait and wait
some more. Surely someone will tell me
what to do.
Time passes.
My neck still aches
from the supersonic dodgeball.

Aren't all your relatives
supposed to greet you
when you get to Heaven?
My two grandfathers should be here.
And Muffin, our family cat
who Dad said was sent to a farm
so he would have a better quality of life,
but I found out later he was hit
by a kid on a skateboard, which can happen, even if
people don't think it can.

If this is the ride of my life,
I want a refund.

No one is coming.
Maybe everyone is somewhere else.
Maybe they are eating in the food court.
Maybe I could get a hot dog-on-a-stick.
My mother never lets me get those
because she once watched a documentary
on how hot dogs are made, and now
will only buy fake dogs, like Soy Pups.

But even if she hadn't seen
that show, she still wouldn't let me eat
one, because of all the calories.
I think my mother truly believes
that all I need is a good makeover
and all my "issues" will go away,
like in those movies where the girl

is really pretty but she wears glasses
and her hair in a ponytail, so you're not
supposed to notice that she's really pretty,
and all she needs to do is let down her hair,
get contacts, and put on some lip gloss
and everyone wants to take her
to the prom, but she decides all she wants
is the nerdy guy who was always nice to her,
so she blows off the captain of the football team
and walks away, her head held high,
to the tune of some pop song.

But you can't take off
twenty extra pounds
by letting down your hair.

II.

I better check that my mother
is really not here
because she has spies
all over the food court,
and I have spent enough time
in my life hearing how I'm ruining
my body by eating junk food.
I don't have to hear it in death.

I head down the hall to Lord & Taylor.
The gate is pulled down, lights off.

If she was at her post
behind the makeup counter,
I'd be able to see her
from here. I suddenly feel a chill
and back up a few feet. The reality
of my situation is sneaking up on me.
I push it away.
What was I thinking of before?
Oh, yeah, the hot dog-on-a-stick.

The escalator is turned off so I climb up it,
which feels weird, like trying to climb up a frozen
    waterfall.
On the counter of the hot dog stand,
on a yellow paper plate, is one
cornbread-covered hot dog-on-a-stick.
Next to it is a Post-it note with my name on it.

I am beginning to feel VERY special!

I gobble the dog, which is just as delicious
as I'd always suspected, only slightly surprised
that I am hungry in Heaven.
As I toss the stick in the plastic garbage bin,
I glance at a wall made of mirrors and gasp.
There is dried, crusty blood all over the right side
of my head and neck and cheek. And my hair
is all matted down, after I spent a particularly long time
straightening it this morning and even burned
my forehead.

That gym floor really made an impact!
I am grossed out by myself.
Totally grossed out.
This is not the first time
I have been horrified at my reflection,
but usually it is because of a pimple on my chin,
or my potbelly or any of the other things
Mom not-so-subtly points out at any opportunity.
Plus, I am still wearing my yellow and green
gym uniform. I do not ever wear yellow
and green in public. In fact, ever since the junior prom
last month, I've worn only black.

I am hideous.
I need to lie down.

The Food Court

I.

I curl up on a bench in front
of Cinnabon and crash.
I sleep the dreamless sleep of the dead.
I never have to get up to pee.
I am awakened by the sound of voices
and the beeping of cash registers.

Only it's not the beeping of cash registers,
it's the beeping of big pieces of medical equipment
attached to various parts of my body.
Through hazy eyes I can see my father pacing
while my mother talks to a man in a white coat.

My heart beats fast at this new development.
I try to speak, but nothing comes out.
I try to move my head, but it does not move.
Instead of the sweet smell of cinnamon rolls
and icing, I smell dried blood and disinfectant.

Well that was definitely the craziest dream.
I can't wait to tell someone about it,
but there's nothing more boring
than listening to someone else's dream,
and I'm short enough on friends these days.

I hear words like "medically induced coma,"
"few days," "do our best," "can't be sure
of the damage." My father puts his head in his hands.
I can see his body shake. "Tessa, Tessa,
my little contessa." He hasn't called me that
since I was five. He hasn't called me much
of anything for a long time, actually. I know
from my limited knowledge of psychology
that the father-daughter relationship is very complex,
but with us it's easy.

He stays out of my way, and I stay out of his.

But he looks so sad now,
and I want to tell him it will be okay.
I'm not dead! Well, not yet anyway.
This should make me happy. I am
pretty sure that I should be ecstatic right now

and I would question my lack of ecstasy
if not for the fact that my nostrils
are filling with a mix of Taco Bell
and chicken teriyaki from Panda Pavilion.
The haze before my eyes clears. I blink
and sit up. I'm not alone anymore.
A group of kids pass my bench,
laughing and pushing each other.

It's daylight at the mall now, and judging
by the crowd, it's lunchtime.
Why am I back here?

You'd think they'd all stare
at a girl with bloody hair.
But no one does.

Am I dreaming again, or is the part
where I'm lying in a hospital bed
the dream, and this really *is* Heaven?
Whoever is in charge here
is not playing nice.

Only one way to find out.
If I'm dreaming, then I should be able
to control my environment.
I am the dreammaker, after all.
I close my eyes and take a deep breath.
Mom can improve her body
with nips and tucks that she thinks

we don't know about,
but I can do the same thing right now.

I focus really hard on making my boobs
grow bigger and bigger,
until I feel them stretch out my t-shirt,
which was already tight to begin with.

"There!" I say triumphantly, opening my eyes.
I look down at what I'm sure will be my new
double Ds, but find my boring ol' B-pluses.
I guess I'm not dreaming.

I am tired of being bounced around.
It's time to take some action.

Mall Manager's Office

I.

I push my way through the glass door.
I shall demand an explanation.
In the Mall of Heaven,
the Mall Manager must be God.

I wait for the receptionist
to acknowledge me.
Cindy never liked me.
I heard her tell Susan in Receiving
that she thought I was trouble.
She doesn't even know me.
Just because once,

I might have taken her parking spot.
It's not like she didn't have an umbrella.

Cindy takes another call instead.
How can she not see my panic,
my confusion? Not to mention
my BLOODY HEAD?
"Helloooo? Am I invisible here?"

"Duh," says a voice behind me.
"You're a slow one, aren't you?
Has anyone spoken to you
since you've been here?"

I turn around to find a tall, thin boy,
a few years older than me,
with a nail sticking out of his head.
Like, a BIG nail. Now THAT'S something
you don't see every day.

II.

My first thought when someone talks to me,
especially a boy, is how to get them to like me.
But then I remember what happened at the junior prom
and how I no longer care about impressing
anyone. Plus, considering my appearance,
I have a greater chance of making someone
run for the hills.

The boy is cute, although one eye
is a little higher than the other,
and of course there's the nail.
But still, I wouldn't kick him out of bed
for eating crackers. I'm not really sure
what that means, since I've never even had a guy
in my bed, so I can't really say what I'd do
with this one, but it seems
like the appropriate reaction.

He tilts his head at me. The nail wobbles.
He has a little silver hoop in the corner
of his eyebrow and I fight the urge
to loop my pinky through it and pull.

"*You're* talking to me," I finally reply.

"Other than me," he says.

I glance over at Cindy. She seems oblivious.
But Nail Boy already seems to know
the answer to his own question
so I change the subject:
"Why do you have a nail in your head?"

He sighs. "If you must know, it's not a nail.
It's a drill bit. I read in a biography
of some British rock star from the sixties
if you drill a hole into your skull, just a little hole,
only to relieve the pressure a bit, you get a rush

like the best drug in the world,
only it isn't bad for you."

I feel no need to point out the obvious.

He grimaces. "True, it didn't turn out as planned.
But enough about me. This is *your* near-death
experience, not mine."

I stop tapping my foot at Cindy
and give him my full attention.
"So I'm having a near-death experience?
I am only *near* death? I am not *dead*?
So I really AM in the hospital?
Like, my body is?"

Nail Boy nods. "You're not very bright, are you?"

This from a boy with a drill bit in his skull.

The roller coaster of emotions
that have been floating around me
are making me feel nauseous.
I'm dead, I'm not dead,
I'm near death. It's too much!

"So tell me, genius, what exactly is going on here?
Is this Heaven, or isn't it? Are *you* dead?
That drill bit looks like it went in pretty far."

"Let's go for a walk, and I'll explain."
He gestures toward the door.

I hesitate. Ever since I was allowed to wander
the halls of the mall alone,
I've been trained not to go off
with strange boys. Especially boys
with nails or drill bits sticking out of their heads.
Still, the usual rules don't seem to apply
here, and I'm pretty sure
I could take him in a fight.

III.

We pass the glass elevator,
where I once got stuck with some crazy guy
who pounded on the doors
when they took too long to open.

We pass the carousel, where I like to go
after the mall closes and it's just us mall brats.
The horse with the unicorn horn is my favorite.

"Where are you taking me?" I ask,
fighting the urge to duck into Hot Topic.

"It's a surprise," he says. "You'll see."

Normally I love surprises.
Anything to break up the routine of life.
But I've had my fill of surprises today.
"So are you, or aren't you?" I ask.

"Am I or am I not what?" he replies,
continuing down the hall, not caring
that he's coming close to knocking
people over.

I roll my eyes. "Dead!"

He shakes his head.

"Are you the Ghost of Christmas Past?
You know, here to show me my evil ways
so I can repent before it's too late?"

He laughs and shakes his head
but doesn't explain further.

I notice the people around me
have taken on a ghost-like quality.
They are thinner, lighter,
than they were before.
This is unnerving.

We pass the rock-climbing wall,
where the boys show off

for the girls and where twice a day
you can win a prize if you climb it the fastest.

We approach the fountain
shaped like a giant gumball machine
where each day of my life (practically)
I've thrown in a coin,
made a wish, the same wish.

I always wish to be someone else.
So far it hasn't come true.

"Need something?" the boy asks,
holding out a dime.

I take it, close my eyes, and toss it
right into the large globe in the center.
"Thanks," I mutter. "I'll pay you back."

"I'm not worried," he says.
"You'll just fish it out
after the mall closes anyway."

I narrow my eyes at him.
How does he know that?

The boy laughs.
It sounds like rain.

Lost and Found

I.

Finally he turns down a long alley
in between stores. My dad's office
is down here, but as a rule,
I do not go down the mall alleys.
Not after The Flasher of '04.
I stop in my tracks.
"Seriously, where are you taking me?"

"Right here," he says, and turns
into the Lost and Found Office.

Rows of lockers line the walls.
I came here once, when I was six,
and my father lost his wallet.
He yelled at the woman
behind the desk until she left in tears,
and my father is not normally
a yeller, but he had just cashed
his paycheck. I've been too embarrassed
to come back in here since then.

To my shock, the woman behind the desk
is the same woman from ten years ago!
There must be dental with this job.
She doesn't look up from her *People* magazine,
just cracks her gum and holds out
her hand. "Key?"

"Uh, are you talking to me?" I ask,
glancing around behind me.

She looks up from her magazine
and repeats, "Key?"

Nail Boy looks at me expectantly.

"What? I don't have any key."

"Look in your pocket," he says.

To humor him, I reach in my pocket
and, lo and behold, pull out a key.
Before I can tell him it's for my gym locker,
he snatches it from me
and hands it to the bored woman.
She turns to the row of lockers,
inserts the key into the last one,
and pulls out a large shopping bag.

She lugs it over to the counter
and makes a big show
of how heavy it is by grunting
as she lifts it up. I can't imagine
what could be in there.

"Here you are," Nail Boy says,
sliding the bag down the counter.
"The stuff you've bought at the mall."

I don't even need to glance at the bag
to know how ridiculous that is.
"I've bought a hundred times more things
in this mall than could possibly be in that bag."

"Ah, but we've chosen the most important."

Hands on my hips, I ask,
"And just who is WE?"

"The Mall Manager, of course."

Figures.

II.

I reach in and pull out the first thing
my hand touches. It is a shoe.
A tiny pink shoe.
I hold it up. "This isn't mine.
I never bought a baby shoe."

"Well, technically your mother bought it.
But the point is, it's yours. The first thing
you ever took home from the mall."
He looks down at my rather large feet.
"My, how you've grown."

I almost chuck the shoe at his head.
But I don't. It feels almost weightless
in the center of my palm.

Nail Boy starts taking each object
out of the bag and lining them up
on the counter.

A Barbie doll in a purple swimsuit
A princess costume
A white fluffy teddy bear with a red bow around the neck

A yellow plastic cup with a daisy on the side
A box of assorted crayons
A hairbrush
A plastic pencil box with Lisa Simpson on it
A small address book with a rainbow on it
A memo pad with my mom's name on it
A glass bowl
A bicycle horn
A *Playboy* magazine
A brown plastic barrette
A sticker that says "I gave today"
A pack of Parliament Menthol Lights
An apron that says "Kiss the Cook"
A red bra
A bear slipper
A red t-shirt
A tube of cheesecake-flavored lip gloss
A turquoise tank top
A pair of pink flip-flops
A roll of toilet paper
A large cookie
A bottle cap
A pair of ski goggles
A light blue prom dress

My eyes open wide at the display.
"Take a good look," he says.

Before me is an odd assortment of my stuff,
most of which I haven't seen or thought of

in years. "What's so special
about these particular things?"

He begins replacing the items in the bag
one by one. "You'll see," he says, cryptic
as ever. He picks up the bag from the counter
and heads toward the door. He walks
so fast I almost have to skip to keep up.
And I do not skip.

He leads me back into the main part of the mall.
"If I were to ask you about your life,"
he says as we walk, "you'd tell me a story.
You'd think it was about you.
But it's not. It never is."

I clutch the shoe harder.
"How could my life story not be my life story?
Who else's would it be?"

He smiles. "It's just a story. One you live in
as the main character. But it's not real."
He holds up the bag. "I'm giving you a chance
to visit the choices you made. The choices
that led you here and –"

"I'm *here* because someone
fired a dodgeball at my head."

"Not quite," he said. "But you'll understand
once you find the answer
to the Big Question you asked yourself."

"What question?"

He pretends not to hear me.
He is not very convincing.

"My college essay question?"

He shakes his head. "Not that one."
He stops in front of Stride Rite.
"Enjoy your first visit to the mall."

"My first visit? More like my millionth."

He flashes another smile,
which at this point no longer
has any charm whatsoever.
Then he turns and walks
toward the shoe store.
I hurry after him.

"Wait! What choices? What question?"
My voice has taken on a desperate tone
usually reserved for trying
to convince my mother I don't
need more foundation.

"Are you my spirit guide?
Are you my Yoda?
What's your name anyway?"

But Nail Boy has already disappeared
inside the store. I mean, really disappeared.
Like, vanished into thin air. He took my bag
with him and has left me holding one tiny pink shoe.

Stride Rite

I hurry to follow him, only to feel
myself pulled back out of the store
as if a giant suction cup has grabbed hold
of my head. I fall hard to the floor,
for the second time in twenty-four hours.
When I look up I see Nail Boy leaning over me.

"Your machine was beeping," he explains,
"so I came over to check.
It's nice to see you awake.
Do you want me to get the nurse?"

"Huh? What's going on?
What's the Big Question

I'm supposed to find the answer to?
Where's all my stuff?"
I try to look around, but I can't move my head.
My hands fly up to my neck.
I have some sort of brace on, keeping
my head immobile. I dart my eyes around.
I don't see the shopping bag
or the Stride Rite
or the mall at all.
I do, however, see white walls,
hospital beds, machines,
And Nail Boy, wearing blue pajamas.

I'm not dead yet.
Again. Or still?
I lay my head back on the pillow
and close my eyes.
This is too much.

"Um, are you okay?" Nail Boy asks.

I shake my head, which doesn't move.
"How come we're back here now?"

"We? Well, I'm here because of this
stupid drill bit stuck in my head
that they can't remove
until some specialist flies into town.
I think you had some kind of accident."

I open my eyes wide.
"You and I weren't just in the mall together?
You don't have a big bag of my things?"
He raises his brows, then shakes his head.

"No Mall Manager,
no Lost and Found?"

He shakes his head.
Drill bit wobbles as usual.

So now he was going to tell me
everything with the mall
didn't really happen? I doubt my imagination
is that good. I say, "But I know
why you have that drill bit in your head."

He nods. "Yeah, I told you
yesterday. I didn't know how
much you could hear. Being
in a coma and all."
He peers at my face.
"Are you okay?"

Now that's the million-dollar question.
"You wouldn't believe
the crazy dream or vision
or near-death experience I had.
And you were in it." I sound like Dorothy
when she gets back from Oz

and tells the farmhands they were there too.
Nail Boy must think I'm still delirious.

"Tell me about it," he says,
sitting on the edge
of the empty bed next to me.

"Really?"

He nods.
So I tell him.
Because like I said,
I'm short on friends
and he has that
cute guy thing going.
Plus someone
must have washed my hair
because the dried blood
is gone.

I tell him the whole thing,
starting with the dodgeball game
and about the *Who Am I* question
and about that bag of my stuff
and about my choices
and some Big Question
and how he disappeared and left me
with an old shoe and no answers.

I look down at my hand, half expecting
to see the shoe. But it's not there. Just a tube
coming out from the inside of my wrist,
which I follow up to a bag
of clear liquid on a pole.

"Drugs?" I ask. " 'Cause I don't think
they're working."

He shakes his head. "Saline water.
So you don't dehydrate.
That tank over there
is feeding you oxygen."

"Fun. How long have I been here?"

"Just since yesterday," he says.

"Have you seen my parents?"

"I think your mom was here.
Thin, a bit manic, lots of hair?"

"That's her."

"Your brother was with her too.
Seemed like a cool guy."

Figures Nail Boy would have
a man-crush on Matt. All the guys

like him, even the straight ones.
"So what do you make of my dream
or vision or near-death experience
or whatever it was?"

"Let me make sure I understand," he says.
"This guy, this 'other me,'
he said that you'd be able to use the stuff
in that bag to find out why you were in Heaven
or the mall or the hospital, or whatever.
Is that right?"

I nod, or try to. I ask,
"Do you know what he meant?
About the Big Question?"

"How should I know?" he replies.
"I'm stupid enough to stick a nail
in my head."

"Drill bit," I correct him.

He walks over to my oxygen
tank and smiles. "Yes. Drill bit."
And then he pulls the plug.

And I try to scream,
but nothing comes out.
And then it ends . . .
and begins.

Stride Rite, Part Two

"Baby don't need shoes!
Baby still can't walk.
Baby is such a big fat baby."
This is my brother talking.
I ignore him. I am too excited.
It's my first real trip to the mall.
Daddy had taken me to Sears once
to get a new washing machine
after Matt put the toaster in it
and turned it on the rinse cycle,
but we never went into the actual mall
itself, so it's not the same thing.

It is everything I dreamed it would be.

I have never seen so many people
in one place. I never knew they came
in so many shapes and sizes.
Each store my parents push me past
has different music coming out of it.
My head swivels back and forth,
trying to soak it all in.

The shoe salesman is very nice to me.
He tickles me under the chin
and says I must be very excited
to be getting my first pair of shoes.

Daddy is looking at shiny daddy-sized shoes
so the salesman sits with me
while my mother goes off
to help Matt find cleats
even though he says he doesn't like sports.
He says he just wants to read comics
but I know he can't read yet.
He's only four.
He acts cooler than he is.
He still sucks his thumb at night.

Finally it's my turn.
The first pair is too tight.
Mom tries to push them on anyway,
says I'm getting too big, too fast.
I'm often "too" something.

Too easily upset. Too loud. Too messy.
Too scared. Too hungry. Too needy.

I am hungry now. I want my bottle.
I make the appropriate sounds.
Mom tells Matt to get Daddy
but Daddy is busy talking
with the pretty lady behind the counter.
Daddy is scruffy and strong
and my Prince Charming.

But then two big people get in line
behind him and I can't see him anymore
or anyone else in my family.
I nearly catapult myself out of my stroller.
First I find Matt under the display table
putting the wrong shoes in the wrong boxes,
then I see Mommy looking in the mirror
sucking in her belly and checking her roots
like she always does when passing her reflection.
I can feel the tears coming, unbidden.
I am no longer interested in the salesman
or his shoes. Everything is too bright and loud
and there is too much space around me.
My back is wet with sweat.

I hear the wailing and realize
it's coming from inside me.
Mommy runs over and grabs the pair of shoes

the salesman is holding
and says, "We'll take these."
He tells her he hasn't tried them
on me yet, and she says it doesn't matter.

That night I am wearing my first pair of shoes.
They feel weird, but my feet feel more solid
on the ground and it occurs to me
I can probably let go of the coffee table
and walk on my own.

Daddy has his video camera out.
This is as good a time as any.
I remove one hand as Matt says,
"Look at ME," and prances
across the floor in his new cleats.
Daddy turns the camera in Matt's direction.
I let go of the table and walk.

Kidz Kuts

I am sitting in the tower
of a pink and white castle
while a huge pair of scissors
are aimed at my head.

Okay, they are not that huge
but they are still sharp and pointy
and headed right toward me.

I wanted the chair shaped like a red fire truck,
but Mommy said that was only for boys.
Plus, I am wearing a pink dress
and Mommy says red and pink together
hurt her eyes.

Needless to say, I am screaming.
I can't even hear the Disney
video on the television in front
of me that is supposed to distract me
from the fact that a part of my body
is about to be taken away.

This is my first real haircut.
I was bald till almost a year old.
Mommy took me to the doctor about it
but he said not to worry.
Mommy wanted to buy me a wig
but Daddy said I was perfect.

Now at two and a half I have hair
past my shoulders but it is very fine
and it tangles and it's not very pretty.
Or so I've heard.

I am waving my beloved Barbie doll
frantically in the air but Mommy grabs my arms
and holds them down. When I am calmer,
she lets go. "Now," she says, but not to me,
"let's see what we can do with this hair."
She lifts a handful of hair and limply lets it drop.
"See?" she says. "No life to it.
How about a perm?"

The hairdresser shakes her head.
"We don't use chemicals with little kids."

I say that I'm not a little kid,
I'm almost three.
The hairdresser smiles politely.

Mommy examines her own hair in the mirror
and then sticks her head next to mine.
"How about," she says, "if you give her
a few highlights? That way mine
will look more natural."

"Bleach is also a chemical," the hairdresser says.

"Fine," Mommy snaps. "Just cut it off, then."

The hairdresser hesitates. "Cut it off?"

"We can't very well leave it like this,"
Mommy says, lifting up a knot.

When we get home Matt points to me
and says, "I got a new brother!"
I am not sure what he means.

Daddy sees me and his eyes widen
but then he says, "Don't you look
beautiful?" I beam and twirl
like the ice skaters on TV with the short hair.

Then Daddy pulls Mommy out of the room.
I'd never heard them fight before.

But now Daddy says,
"Are you trying to turn her into a tomboy?"
And Mommy says, "I don't think
she's going to be a beauty queen. At least
she won't look so messy all the time."
And Daddy says, "Do you want to turn
into your own mother? Criticizing
your daughter all the time?"
And that is apparently a bad thing
to say because Mommy's face turns red
and Daddy tells her she's going to give me
a complex if she doesn't stop.

I don't know what a complex is,
but I don't like the sound of it.
Mommy and Daddy are still fighting
so I slip into their room
and steal the scissors from the drawer.

It takes a few minutes to get the hang of the scissors,
but then I snip every hair off of Barbie's head,
and then tend to my other dolls
until they look just like me.
I bring them all downstairs
and line them up on the couch.

Matt hoots and Mommy puts me
in a very long time-out.
I stare blankly at the wall,

not thinking of anything,
just feeling the air
on the back of my neck.

The Halloween Store

The winner of the best Halloween costume
gets a pumpkin that lights up.
I really want that pumpkin.

The whole preschool wants that pumpkin.
Next year, in kindergarten,
I heard the winner gets a pumpkin
that not only lights up,
but talks too!

But for now, I'll settle for one
that just lights up.
I told Mommy that I really need
a great costume this year.
Last year I was a princess

and I hated the frilly dress and tights
and half the other girls were princesses.
This year I want to be an elf.

My teacher, Miss Rudder, taught us
that Halloween isn't just about the candy.
It's also about make-believe. On Halloween
we can be anything we want to be.
She said we can be anything we want
every other day too.

The Halloween store in the mall
is only there for two months,
then it becomes the Christmas store,
and other times it's nothing at all.

The woman who greets us at the door
is dressed like a sheep. Cobwebs crisscross
the corners and pumpkins with candles
inside them flicker on high shelves.

I see a little boy crying in the corner
but no one else seems to notice. I pull
on Mommy's arm to show her,
but she tells me to go with Daddy,
that she'll catch up. She goes off
to the grown-up section and I see her
looking at a maid's uniform,
which is weird because I've never seen her
clean anything.

Daddy is crabby today. A pretty mom walks by
but he doesn't even look. I put my hand
in his, but I don't think he notices. Mommy says
he had a bad day at work but I'm not really sure
what he does at work.

Daddy keeps pulling costumes off the rack
that are either too big or too small for me.
Mommy comes over and grabs a princess
costume and marches to the counter with it.
"Noooooo . . . ," I whine, following her.
"I don't want that one. I want to be an elf.
Matt gets to be whatever HE wants!"
Which is always a sports player.

"There are no elf outfits," Mommy says.
But I don't think she even looked.

It is freezing the day of the Halloween parade
and we're all in heavy coats. Half of us
are princesses but no one can see our costumes
anyway. The lace collar is itching me
something fierce. All anyone can see
is my stupid tiara. Amanda Jentis wins.
She is an elf.
I try not to cry.

I think Miss Rudder was wrong.
I don't think you *can* be anything
you want to be.

elementary school

KB Toy & Hobby

"That one," I say, pointing to the bear
on the top shelf. I choose him because
he looks sad sitting on the shelf
with all the other bears,
with one of his eyes
focusing sort of downward, and maybe
no one will buy him because he is slightly "off."
He is soft and white with a shiny red ribbon
that curls up on both ends.

"He looks demented," Matt says
when we get home. But he is just jealous
that Nana took me to the mall and not him.
The newly named Fuzzy McFuzz

is my new best friend and nothing
Matt could say matters.

After dinner Mommy and Daddy and Matt
go to see Matt pitch. I am never invited
to the Little League games so Nana
stays with me. When they all come home,
they smell like cotton candy.

When I wake up the next morning
I go running into my parents' room.
Fuzzy McFuzz is gone! Vanished in the night!
Daddy hugs me as I sob and Mommy crawls
under beds and into the backs of closets.
Even Matt opens a dresser drawer or two.

And sometime during the search
I remember where he is.
I left him in Nana's car
when I climbed into the backseat
to say goodbye. But it occurs to me
that I haven't had this much attention
since I fell on the playground
and my tooth went through my lip.

So I don't tell them. I just sniffle.

The search continues through the day.
I am given extra fries at dinner.

The next day at breakfast
we hold a memorial service. We go around
the table and all say nice things about Fuzzy.
Mommy says he was very handsome for a bear.
Daddy says he liked his sense of humor.
Matt says he smelled good, and that was sweet
of him because I didn't think anyone
noticed that I had dabbed some
of Dad's old aftershave on Fuzzy's nose.

When it is my turn, part of me wants to say
it's okay, that Fuzzy is just on a trip
and he'll be back the next time
Nana comes to visit. But another part of me
just wants to cry, so that's what I do.

Daddy offers to buy me a new bear
but I say no. So he gives me a plastic ring
with a picture of Wonder Woman
on it, which he says he had been saving
for my Christmas stocking.
Daddy says Wonder Woman is a superhero
who is very brave and that I have been brave,
so he thought I should have it now.

I don't know what the right word would be
for what I have been, but I'm pretty sure
brave isn't it.

Party City

Mommy wants to get red cups
but I think yellow is more
appropriate. Who wants to drink
lemonade out of red cups?
It just doesn't make sense.
Plus the yellow ones have a picture
of a daisy on them, and I love daisies.

She had said the whole lemonade stand
could be my project, under my control,
so she lets me buy the yellow cups.

It's not like I really want to sell
lemonade, but everyone at school

has to do it and the money goes to whatever
charity my class agrees on. I voted to give it
to the animal shelter because last month
they put a poster up in the mall with a kitty
who only has three legs.
Daddy took me to visit the cat because I begged
and begged, but we can't get him
because Mom bought all white furniture
after Muffin went to live on that farm.
The people at the shelter said
I can visit him anytime I want
unless he gets adopted, and I've gone
twice more already.

But my class votes to put the money
toward getting new chairs in the auditorium
because the old ones are really, really hard
and hurt your butt to sit on,
so I can understand their point.

I am secretly planning on giving
some of mine to the three-legged cat anyway.
I'm sure I'll do so well that there will be
enough to share. After all, my mom
makes excellent lemonade from fresh
lemons, while I happen to know
most of the other kids are using powder,
which is really just a bunch of chemicals
with no actual lemon in it.

Daddy drags a square card table
to the corner of our driveway
and I unfold a lawn chair.
I had already made a big poster
so I tape it to the edge of the table
and it looks very professional,
like a real artist did it, not a kid.

Mommy brings out the lemonade
and the ice cubes clink against the side
of the pitcher and the sky above is blue
with no clouds at all and there is a nice breeze
and I am wearing a pretty yellow hat
and I think that even if Matt were to be
really obnoxious to me today, even that
couldn't bring me down.

The first car that comes by is filled
with a family who all smile at me,
but the car keeps going. I smile back.
After all, maybe they weren't thirsty.

By the time the eighth car passes,
my good mood is starting to fade.
A fly keeps circling the edge of the pitcher
and I have to keep swatting it, and once
I spilled a little on my hand and now it's all sticky
whenever I touch something. My hat blows
off into the street, where it lands directly

in a trickle of muddy water, the only reminder
on the whole street of last night's rain.

The fly finally dive-bombs into the pitcher
and Mommy has to make me a whole
new one. The new one doesn't have any ice
because she said she's not wasting more ice
on lemonade that no one's buying.

The cars keep passing.
I have now begun to stick my tongue out
at them. I don't even wait
until they have fully passed by.

At five o'clock Mommy comes out
and tells me we have to pick up Matt
at soccer practice. One more car approaches
and it actually slows down.
"How much?" the lady asks.
"Fifty cents," I tell her,
already grabbing a cup off the stack.

"Nah," she says, shaking her head.
She drives off and I go running
after the car even though I know better
than to run into the road.
"It's for charity!" I yell. "Charity!"
But she doesn't slow down.

I fume in the car on the way to get Matt
and I never go to visit the three-legged cat
again. I don't know if it died
or ever got adopted but every time I sit
in the new plush auditorium seats,
my stomach hurts.

Michael's Arts and Crafts

For Thanksgiving we all have to draw
the scene where the Indians are having lunch
with the Pilgrims, except my art teacher, Mrs. Eisen,
calls them "Native Americans" and "Settlers."

I love art class and the way the crayons feel
slippery in my hands and the way the pile of them
on the table looks like a broken-up rainbow.
I am annoyed that Hailey Briggs keeps
hogging the green one, but Mommy always says
I am too easily angered and need to count
to ten before I act rashly,
and that I have to learn to wait my turn.

So I wait for her to finish, which seems like forever,
because she is making everything green.
The corn, the Settlers' clothes, everything.
Finally she lays down the green crayon
and I can do my grass.
Each blade has to look
like it can really bend in the wind.
I must have pressed too hard,
because the crayon breaks in my hand.
I look at my classmates. Everyone is busy working.
Mrs. Eisen is across the room. I make a decision
that doesn't even feel like a decision.
I push the two ends of the crayon together,
hard, and they stick. Gently,
I lay the crayon back in the pile
and pick up the yellow one.

A few minutes later Hailey takes the green crayon
again, and it breaks in her hand.
Mrs. Eisen is standing over us
at the time and sees. She tells Hailey
that she must replace that crayon
from her own collection,
which she well knows is the punishment
for breaking a crayon.
Hailey starts crying that it wasn't her fault,
but Mrs. Eisen lectures her on lying.
I keep my eyes down, focused on coloring in my sun.

That day after school I feel kind of bad about what
  happened
because even though Hailey shouldn't have been hogging
  the crayon,
she did gave me half of her Twinkie at lunch last week,
which my mom would never have let me have
because she says if I keep eating
the way I do, I'll be known as "the fat kid"
in school and get picked on.

So while I'm at the mall waiting
for Mom's shift to end,
I buy a new box of crayons
with my allowance.
This box has some really cool colors
like Whisper Silver and Azure Blue.
I figure I will give Hailey the whole box
and not just the green one
(even though there are all these cool new colors)
but when we get to school
Hailey sides up to me
just as I'm reaching into my book bag
and she says, "I know it was you
who broke that crayon.
Maybe you should have eaten it instead!"

And I'm not sure
if she is calling me fat
or maybe she is just saying

I should have gotten rid of the evidence.
Either way, I remove my hand from my bag
and I don't say anything because my apology
is stuck in my throat.

Later, in art class, I paint Whisper Silver clouds
and Azure Blue skies and Mrs. Eisen compliments me
on my creative use of color, and on Thanksgiving,
Dad puts the picture up on the fridge
and everyone says the sky with its silver clouds
is the best part.

And I think how strange it is
that if that whole thing with the crayon
hadn't happened, my sky wouldn't have looked
nearly this good. I sense this
says something important about life,
but I can't figure out what it is.

Lord & Taylor

Mom brags that she can tell her customers
what shades of makeup
would look best on them
just by hearing their voice.

I don't know if this is true,
but she does have a lot of loyal customers
who rely on her to tell them
if their T-zone is dry or oily.
I am probably the only second-grader
in my entire school
who knows what a T-zone is.

I tell her I need the perfect gift to bring
to Suzy Holmdel's birthday party.

Mom asks me what Suzy looks like,
and I tell her she is the tallest kid in our class
and has red hair with a braid sometimes,
and Mom says, "Is her hair thick or thin?"
And I say, "I have no idea. Thick, I guess."
And she says, "You can't go wrong
with a good hairbrush. Every girl
should have one." And I say, "A *hairbrush*?
I'm sure she has one already."

"Yes, but not the *right* one. I'll pick one
up at the store tomorrow."
I can't seem to convince her
to just buy Suzy a CD or video
or stuffed animal like everyone else
will be giving her.

I wrap the brush really nicely, figuring
if she doesn't like it, then at least she will
like the wrapping, but when we get to the party
I slip the package on the bottom of the gift pile
just to be on the safe side.

There are cupcakes with Suzy's picture on them
and a magician who pulls all sorts of things
out of Suzy's ears, like a dollar bill
and a pretzel and a rose,
but no one really talks to me very much.
I hear Hailey Briggs ask this girl Jessica
(who I've never spoken a word to)

why I was even invited, and Jessica says
because the whole class was invited.

When it is time for the presents,
Suzy's mom moves the whole pile from the table
and puts it in front of Suzy on the floor,
so now my gift is on the top.

Suzy rips open the wrapping
without even taking the time to see
how pretty it is or how much effort it took
to make sure the bow was curled evenly.
When she gets to the brush,
she glances at it with an expression I can't decipher,
then tosses it aside and reaches
for the next gift. It's not like she laughed at it,
so maybe Mom was right and she liked it,
and at least no one knew it was from me,
so that is a relief.

The rest of the gifts are videos
and CDs
and stuffed animals
and the occasional bracelet
or earrings
or toy
and I think maybe giving a gift
that no one else did
was kind of cool after all.

But then while we're waiting for our mothers
to pick us up, Hailey tells Jessica
she thinks I was the one who gave Suzy the hairbrush
and wasn't that the weirdest gift
and was I trying to tell her she needs
to brush her hair more?

And before I can think,
the Hawaiian Punch I am holding just happens
to slip out of my hand and on top of Hailey's head,
and I probably won't get invited
to any more birthday parties for a while,
which is fine by me because I know
it's impossible to pull a flower
out of someone's ear.

Spencer's

Mom doesn't let me shop
at Spencer's but I stop to look
in the window and see Matt
in there goofing around with his friends
and he sees me see him.

I can tell he is weighing his options.
Hide, and hope I didn't really see him,
not hide, and hope I don't tell Mom,
or wave me in. Our eyes meet.
He waves me in.

I don't understand what most of the stuff
in this store is all about,

but there's a whole section
on the *Simpsons* TV show,
which I'm not really supposed to watch,
but Mom and Dad usually aren't home
until after it's over.

I need a pencil case for third grade
and I ask Matt to buy me one
with Lisa Simpson on it,
and even though he grumbles and complains,
he buys it anyway.
Later I heard him tell Mom
that it came from somewhere else.

I feel very grown up
with my new pencil case.
Everyone knows how smart
and mature Lisa Simpson is, so now
I kind of feel like her,
and we're the same age too.

The night before school
starts, I line my pens and pencils
up neatly and then one by one
I put the exact right number
(seven) into the box
so they won't slide around.

I even have room for an eraser
on top, so I put in my red one
that smells like cherries.

I love the desk I'm assigned.
It's right next to Stefanie Gold
who always has Frosted Flakes
in a little baggie in her desk.

Stefanie and I have a lot in common.
We both have mothers who made us go
to fat camp for a month this past summer,
which was really like a regular
day camp except we ran around
more and had carrots instead
of ice cream for snacks.

We both only lost five pounds
the whole summer, and we both said
we didn't care.

We both like cats over dogs,
magazines over books,
and television over movies.

She has one sister
and I have one brother,
but she said that her sister
is her best friend
and for the first time

I realized that my brother and I
weren't friends at all.

The one annoying thing about Stefanie
is that she got the same pencil case
as I did, even though she knew
I had it first. And hers is filled
with those cool new gel pens
in all different colors, and I only have one
gel pen, which is pink,
and it's almost used up.

On the fourth day of school I notice
one of the pencils in my case
is missing. I look inside my desk,
and underneath, and I ask everyone
around me but no one has seen it,
and it's not like I care so much
about the pencil itself
because it was just an ordinary yellow #2,
but now the rest of the pens and pencils
in my box are rolling around.

When Stefanie leaves to go to the bathroom,
I happen to notice all of her pens
lined up so nicely and I tell myself
she has so many pens and won't notice
one missing. I tell myself it's only fair
because she copied me and bought the same pencil case,

even though my mother says that imitation
is the highest form of flattery.

I reach over and grab
a purple gel pen
and stick it in my sock.
I know nobody sees me because everyone else
is watching a movie about fire safety
and the importance of stop, drop, and roll.

Stefanie returns to her desk,
and it's like she knows something
is wrong because she's instantly like,
"Where's my purple gel pen?" and then she turns to me,
of all people, her closest friend here,
and shoots me daggers.

Then she starts crying and Ms. Anderson
calls her up to her desk and Stefanie points to me
and then Ms. Anderson calls ME up to her desk
and says, "Tessa, have you seen
Stefanie's pen?" and I say, "No, I have not."

She asks me if I'm sure. Heart pounding,
I say yes, certain they can see the bulge
in my sock. "Keep an eye out for it," she says,
and I promise to do just that
and Stefanie weepily apologizes
for accusing me and gives me some Frosted Flakes.

And when she offers up the bag
and I stick my hand in and scoop
up some Flakes, I realize I'm the kind of person
who steals things from their friends
and I better not let anyone know me too well
in case they find out
what else I'm capable of.

I wait till I get home to take the pen out
of my sock. Then I find an old notebook
of Matt's from when he was in second grade
and I write all over it in the purple pen
for almost an hour until all the ink has run out,
and then I throw it in the garbage
so now, even though she doesn't know it,
Stefanie wouldn't want that old pen anyway.

Hallmark

Somehow while I wasn't looking
all the girls got autograph books,
but I didn't know I was supposed
to get one, so during the last week
of school, I am the only one in my class
who has nothing for anyone to write
their names in, and *BFF* and *2Good2Btrue*
and *have a great summer.*

So I look everywhere for an autograph
book but they are all sold out because
everyone already has one so I'm stuck
buying an address book instead.

I go up to everyone and ask for their
phone number, and in a way I feel
kind of important, because no one
else has everyone's phone number,
and Jessica, who lives down the street
from me, says, "Why would I tell you
my phone number? It's not like
I want you to call me."

So that night at home I am looking
through the address book
and when I come to where Jessica's name would be
I get really mad because I don't know
why she wouldn't want me to call her
just because she may have gotten splashed
with that Hawaiian punch that I spilled
on her friend Hailey last year.

I look up her number in our big phone book,
so now I have it anyway.

When I am closing the phone book
I see instructions on calling the fire department
and before I can stop myself, I am calling
and telling them there is a fire at this Jessica's house
and not five minutes later I hear the sirens
and about ten minutes after that our phone rings
and my dad gets it and it's the fire chief
and he wants to talk to me and my father is fuming

and the fire chief says, "Calling in a false alarm
is a federal offense."

But honestly, I don't see what the huge deal
is, after all the fire station is right down the street,
until he says, "And what if there was a real fire
somewhere, like at YOUR house, and we couldn't
get to it because our truck was out on a false alarm?"

He tells me I will have to present a speech
on fire safety to my class next year
and I tell him that we already learned
about stop, drop, and roll, and he says
he doesn't care, we'll just have to learn it again.

My parents almost never punish me
and I heard my aunt once ask why,
and my mom said they work so late
that when they get home
they don't want to yell all the time.

I have no problem with this arrangement.

So the only thing that happens to me
is I'm not allowed to use the phone
for a week. It's not like I have anyone
to call anyway.

Things Remembered

I never know what to get
my mom for her birthday.
Dad always gets her makeup
or clothes or jewelry and I can't
really afford any of those things.
Now it's her birthday and I haven't
gotten her anything and neither has Matt
and Dad is annoyed.

He warns us that this birthday
is going to be particularly hard
on Mom and suggests that Matt and I
go in on something special together. I know
Dad's saying this in the hopes that we will
get along better if we have to spend time together,

but he doesn't understand that four years
is just too big a difference, especially if one of us
is good-looking and smart and athletic and popular
and one of us isn't.

I go into Mom's room to tell her
Matt and I are going out for a while
and I find her in bed,
her head under the blanket
like a little kid hiding from her parents.
This is very unlike her. She is always
the first one up, and by the time the rest stumble
into the kitchen for breakfast,
she has already run five miles,
done a hundred sit-ups, and has a full face
of makeup on.

"Mom?" I ask, lifting a corner
of the blanket to peer under.
"Are you all right?"

She mumbles something
about turning forty and the best years
of her life are gone
and she'll never look young again
and how I wouldn't understand
because I'm only nine
and pulls the blanket back over her.
Looks like Dad was right
about Mom and her birthday.

We go to the mall
and decide to get Mom stationery
that says, "From the desk of Valerie Reynolds"
and I get to pick out the color of the ink
and the font and whether the words go on
the top of the paper or the bottom.

I wrap the stationery up really well
(except for a few pieces that I keep
because they were the ones we tried out
different fonts on, and I think
they look cool with her name written
all these different ways) and Matt
uses his computer to make a card
to go with it, and we both sign it,
and it's almost like we're friends
or something.
Maybe Dad had the right idea.

That afternoon my new next-door neighbor Naomi
comes over to play. She is a year older
than me and she used to live in New York City
except she calls it "The City."

Naomi knows things.
She knows all the curse words,
and some hand gestures too.
I have learned a lot from her.

I can tell she's getting bored,
playing with my stupid toys.
I look out the big window
in our playroom and see Jessica
riding bikes with Hailey Briggs,
and an idea forms in my brain
that I know Naomi will appreciate.

I run to my desk and grab
some paper and a black-tip pen
and run back to the playroom,
where Naomi scrawls out the words,
"Fuch you," and then she folds it up
into a tiny square. Without putting our shoes on,
we run outside and give it to Jessica
and say, "Someone told us to give this to you"
and then we run away
before she can even say anything.
Naomi gives me a high five
and heads back to her house
and I feel really energized,
like I drank too much soda.

Mom finally gets out of bed in time
to eat the dinner that Dad has made
for her (burnt chicken that we all had
to pretend was delicious).
I am helping to load the dishwasher
when the doorbell rings. Mom says, "Maybe
someone sent me flowers"

in a voice that clearly means,
"Someone better have sent me flowers."
But it must not have been flowers
because after a minute she calls me into the hall.
Jessica and Hailey and their moms
are there and for a split second I have no idea
why, and then I remember.

But then I think, they can't prove
it was me. After all, it wasn't even my handwriting.

My mom hands me the note and says,
"Did you write this?" and I say no,
so she hands it back to Jessica's mom
and says, "Sorry we can't help you,"
and then Jessica's mom says, "Turn
the note over," so my mom does,
and it says *From the desk of Valerie Reynolds*
over and over again in different colors
and sizes.

She says, "I've never seen that before,"
and at this point, Matt has turned off
whatever violent video game he was playing
to see what all the commotion is about,
and he sees the stationery and he glares at me
for ruining the surprise just an hour before
we were going to give her the present,
and then he turns the paper over,
reads what we wrote,

and starts laughing. "You spelled it wrong,"
he says, which is really embarrassing
because I pride myself on being the best speller
in my class and I hadn't noticed that Naomi
had spelled it wrong, but even still,
I wouldn't have known how to spell it right anyway.

But Matt is the only one laughing.
I have to apologize to Jessica
and Hailey and to their moms,
and I am not given any birthday cake
and I bet my mom is glad
to have an excuse
not to give me any.

But later that night
when everyone is asleep, I take some
from the fridge, only it tastes really bad,
and I find out later that Matt had lifted up
the icing and put mustard underneath
because he knew I would try to sneak some.

Crate and Barrel

Mrs. Robins does not joke around.
She has no sense of humor
at all. So when Tim Jones pretends
to drop his science project out the window,
but it slips and falls for real,
she gives him an F on it, and now
we all have to do an extra project
for the year or else we won't move
on to fifth grade.

I had wanted to do mine on why
a bag of cotton candy, if left under the bed
all night, turns into a flat sheet
of sugar by morning, which is exactly what happened
to me after the Kiwanis Carnival

last month, but Mrs. Robins says it has to be
more scientific than that.

She also won't let me find out
how long it takes a Twinkie
to explode in the microwave,
or if Coca-Cola can effectively clean
a hopscotch board made of chalk
off of my driveway.

I wind up doing the same project
Matt did in fourth grade –
trying to see if an egg can bounce.

I'm not alone though. Rick Vinik
is doing the same thing. In the back
of our classroom we both have one egg
soaking in water for a week, and one
in vinegar. The shell on the one
in the vinegar is supposed to disappear
and the inner layer is supposed to get
all rubbery so it bounces. At least
that's how I remember it when Matt did it,
even though I was only in first grade.

I had to go to Crate and Barrel to get
the thick glass bowls I needed
for the eggs because Mom wouldn't let me
leave one of ours at school,
because apparently Matt forgot

to bring his home and that was the bowl
she used to put boiling water into
to steam her face at the end of the day.

I don't think it's fair that I had to spend
my allowance on a school project
just because Matt messed up,
but there is no convincing my mother
of anything, so I bought the cheapest ones.

On the day our report is due,
I arrive in the classroom first.
As expected, both of the eggs
in the bowls of water look
just like they did that first day.

Rick's vinegar egg looks very rubbery,
but mine doesn't look so good.
Maybe the vinegar that mom gave me,
which we had used last month to dye
Easter eggs, wasn't the right kind.

I glance once at the door,
then I lift the egg out of his bowl
and switch it with mine.
I have long ago accepted the fact
that I am the kind of person
who does things like this,
so in a very real way,
it doesn't even feel wrong.

I bounce my (his) egg in front
of the whole class and get an A.
His (my) egg just lies there on the floor.
He winds up getting an A
too, because the point was to run
an experiment and to come up
with a conclusion, not whether the egg
actually bounced.

Still, I'm really glad mine bounced.

Modell's Sporting Goods

When the rubber ball at the end
of my old bike horn cracks,
Mom says I can choose another
one. I'm examining all the ones
on the shelf, and trying them out,
and she says I'm giving her a migraine
and to please just choose one.

With the streamers at the end
of my handlebars and my big new horn
and the playing cards stuck
in the spokes of my wheels
that make my bike sound like a motorcycle,
I am the queen of the neighborhood.
Everyone can hear me coming.

Naomi and I like to ride our bikes
through the neighborhood until we get lost.
Well, really we just pretend
we're lost because we're not allowed
to go farther than three blocks
in any direction from our houses.

Today we leave our bikes
in front of the park and walk
to the other end of it, which is nowhere
I've been before but Naomi has
and she says she wants to show me
something and I'm still sort of shocked
that someone older and so worldly
is willing to hang out with me,
so I happily go along.

And there, in front of us,
is this perfect pond. It is perfectly
round and perfectly green
and perfectly hidden
from all the moms and babies
playing in the park.

Before I know it, Naomi has taken off
her shorts and t-shirt and tossed them
in a pile and is running
into the pond in just her Keds
and her pink underpants.

I run in after her, but I don't take
anything off because I didn't think
anyone would see my underpants today
and I'm wearing an old pair of Matt's,
which happen to be his Superman pair.

One of the things I like about Naomi
is that she doesn't say,
"Oh, you're such a chicken, you didn't
take off your clothes." She just says,
"Isn't this great?" and it *is* great.

I love being in water because it feels
like air, except heavier
than the air ever really is,
and floating on the water
feels like flying.

That night at dinner, Mom tells Dad
that Naomi's father went to something
called a *happy hour,* which doesn't sound
like a bad thing to me, but apparently it is
if you're a family man, and he drove
his car straight up their driveway,
into their garage, and then kept going
right through their living room and out
into the backyard.

Matt and I run to the window and sure
enough, we can see the front end

of their SUV sticking out of the house.
Dad lectures us on the evils of drinking
and driving as though it's not going to be years
and years until I'm able to drive.

"The one I feel sorry for,"
says Mom, "is that little girl."

"Naomi?" I ask, surprised
that anyone should feel sorry
for Naomi, who as far as I could tell
was the coolest girl on the planet.
Mom gives me her exasperated look.
The one that means, I'm supposed
to understand things better than I do.
Then she says, "She didn't ask
for a father who's a drunk."

"Valerie!" my father says.
"The man had a few drinks
and you crucify him."

This is the point
where Matt and I slink
away from the table
unnoticed.

After dinner I ride my bike
in front of Naomi's house
and honk my new horn.

Naomi comes running out, and she runs
right past the police car in her driveway
and she hops on her bike and says,
"Let's go."

We ride around the block and I wonder
if we're going to go back to the pond,
but we don't.

She stares straight ahead
at the road in front of her,
like she hopes it will suddenly lead
to somewhere else.

I feel like I'm supposed to say
something, but I've never been
in this situation before, so I ride
up beside her and say,
"I'm sorry your dad is a drunk."

She drags her sneakers along the road
until her bike stops. She starts to cry
and says, "Only babies put playing cards
in the spokes of their wheels."

She hops back on her bike and I look
down at the cards stuck in my spokes
and I yank them out and shove them
in my pocket. Maybe it's not such a bad thing
if no one hears me coming.

Brentano's

Matt and I are waiting for Mom
to close up her makeup counter,
so as usual we wander over
to the bookstore next door. No one minds
if you browse and don't buy,
and the manager, a jolly woman named Millie,
always gives us Juicy Fruit.

Millie asks us to watch the front
of the store while she runs
to the bathroom in the back,
and we say no problem. While I immerse
myself in an issue of *Teen*
even though I'm not one yet, I see
out of the corner of my eye

that Matt is stealing
a *Playboy* from behind the counter.

I watch him push it deep into his backpack
and I don't say anything because I love the fact
that I caught him doing something wrong,
and that's even better than telling on him for it.
The next day I am in the middle of a test
on one-celled organisms when the student teacher,
Ms. Whelan, grabs the sheet off my desk
and loudly accuses me of looking
at my neighbor's answers.

"I didn't," I tell her. "I swear."

Everyone looks up and I can feel
my face starting to flush. Why would I cheat
off a kid who got a C on the last test?

She puts my test back on my desk
and says, "I'm watching you."
A few giggles from my classmates later,
I have a plan to exact my revenge.
After school, while Matt is out
in the backyard sprinting from
one tree to the next and timing himself,
I sneak into his room
and quickly find the *Playboy*
under his mattress.
Matt has bent back some of the pages

and I have to look closely to discover
what makes one naked woman
different from another. I learn that
breasts come in three sizes – big, bigger,
and huge, and that I'll likely never
be a candidate for *Playboy*
because they are all skinny and
the only compliment I ever get
on my appearance is when people say
I have a pretty face,
which is what they always say
when you're chubby.

I take a pair of scissors and carefully cut
out a few of the women, but only from the neck
down. Then I open
my school newspaper, turn to the photo
of the fourth grade spring picnic, and cut out
Ms. Whelan's head.

I place her head on top of each body
until I find one that matches in size and coloring.
I tape her head onto the matching body
and then carefully, respectfully, stick
the rest of the women back into the magazine.

As I put it back where I found it, I have to laugh
because when Matt finds it, he won't be able
to do anything about it without letting everyone know
he stole it in the first place.

The next day I place my creation in an envelope
and leave it on Ms. Whelan's desk before
the rest of the class files in.

In my hurry to get to school I forgot
to go to the bathroom this morning,
and even though I don't want to miss
Ms. Whelan's face when she opens my letter,
I can't hold it in any longer.

I rush down the hall and am about
to crash through the door of the bathroom
when I almost trip on a first-grade boy
sitting on the floor, crying.
I try to walk past him, but he keeps sniffling
louder, so I sigh and turn back
and ask him what's the matter.

He doesn't answer me, but he has the biggest,
roundest, most owl-like eyes
I've ever seen. He reminds me
of a stuffed animal I used to have
even though it was a bear, and not an owl.

No one else is in the hall now,
so I help him up and bring him
to the office and hand him over
to one of the secretaries, who says, "Aren't you
a good girl," and I wonder how she can't see
that he is clearly a boy.

By the time I get back to class,
it is too late. I immediately recognize
my letter torn into pieces on the top
of the trash can. I guess it is for the best
because suddenly I don't feel very angry
anymore.

Claire's

Eliza Rosenberg has the coolest hair
in the whole fifth grade. It looks like a sheet
of light brown water flowing off her head.

She sits in front of me
and it's very tempting to touch it,
but I don't want her to think I'm weird
because we've started sitting together
at lunch, and I don't want to ruin it.

Eliza has a lot of friends
but they are all in the other
fifth-grade class, and she has chosen
me, out of everyone, to hang out with.
It might be because next to me

and my frizzy hair
she looks even better,
and I don't care
if that's the reason, I'm just glad.

It's only the second week of school
and we don't know each other that well
yet, but after school today her mom is bringing
us to the mall, which is great because I'll be able
to show her things I bet she hasn't seen.

Eliza's mom says she doesn't
want us to walk around on our own,
even though I explain that I practically live
at the mall and know people who work
in every store and it's totally safe.
But she said she'll wait
for us outside of each store,
which is almost as good.

Stefanie was going to come
with us, but her mother signed
her up for a kids' after-school version
of Weight Watchers, which I'm really glad
my mother doesn't know about,
and I'm not going to tell.

Even though Stefanie would be
my best friend if she wasn't best friends

with her sister, I'm glad she's not
here, because now I don't have to share Eliza.

First we go into the bulk candy store
and fill our little paper bags
with Runts, mini-jawbreakers,
caramel squares, gumballs, and candy
corn, which isn't as good as the candy corn
they get in around Halloween,
but it's still really good.

I'm not supposed to go into this store
because of my tendency to put on weight
if I even look at junk food, but Carolyn,
who weighs the candy behind the counter,
says that kids my age aren't supposed
to be worried about such things, and I tell her
she doesn't have my mother, who usually makes me
something different for dinner
than the rest of the family.

Eliza starts to stick her hand
into the tutti-fruitti Jelly Belly bin,
but I stop her just like Carolyn
would have stopped someone
from stealing at my mom's makeup counter.

Then we put quarters into
the massage chairs in the center
of the mall that give you a back massage

from inside the chair somehow.
They don't like children to use them,
but they make exceptions for us mall brats
and our friends.

We pass the bungee trampolines,
and Eliza says she's never been
on them, and I don't want to tell her
that I haven't either, so I say,
"Oh, you've gotta try it, it's really fun,"
and she says she will if I will,
and her mother says okay,
so we wait in line and pay our two dollars.

The guy ties these straps around our waists
and wrists and attaches the other ends to these really
tall poles. We climb up onto the trampolines
and look at each other and then bounce
and bounce until we're doing flips in the air
and not even on purpose, that's just what happens.

For a minute I forget everything else
and just fly. Not since swimming
in the pond with Naomi have I felt
this way.
      Special.   Free.
        Chosen.

When our turn is over, Eliza's mother
(who watched from twenty feet away)

shakes her head as if she knows
we're going to ask her
if we can do it again.

So Eliza and I go into my favorite store,
Claire's. We try on bracelets and hats
and Eliza slings six pocketbooks
on her shoulders at once. All I can afford
is a plain brown plastic barrette,
but Eliza gets this really cool one
with rhinestone fish on it.

She wears it to school the next day
and flips her hair around even more
than usual. Everyone ooohs and ahhhs
as the rhinestones glisten under
the fluorescent lights and everyone
says what a pretty barrette it is.

Sometime during Mrs. Simon's lecture
on the Civil War, I find myself consumed
with watching that fish barrette slowly slip down
Eliza's hair, which is too soft and shiny
to hold it in place very long.

By the time Mrs. Simon has finished
telling us that if we don't learn
from history, we are doomed to repeat it,
the barrette has fallen out of her hair
and is resting on the top of my desk.

I cup my hand over it, and slide it
along the length of my desk,
and into my pocket.

When we leave for recess,
I drop it in the trash bin
so that when Eliza realizes
she lost it, which should be soon,
I can be the one to find it.

During recess we do the usual:
blow big bubbles, play hopscotch,
whisper about who in our class
wears a bra already, and dare
each other to kiss Michael Parks.
She doesn't mention her barrette.

When we get back to the room,
I walk by the trash can, ready
to casually retrieve the barrette,
but the trash is gone! The janitor
must have emptied it! My stomach
twists into a huge knot.

We're on different buses
so I don't get to see if Eliza notices
the barrette is missing on the way home.
I stare out the window,
watch the town go by,

and pop the last of the bulk candy
into my mouth.

But instead of the momentary thrill
I would normally get from eating
chocolate and sugar and chocolate-covered sugar,
it all tastes like cardboard.

Bloodmobile

I am getting ready for school
when I hear my mother yelling,
"OMYGOD OMYGOD."
At first I think she must have broken
a nail or something
equally earth-shattering
but then I see my father racing down
the stairs and then I hear *him* say,
"OMYGOD." I run down to find
them in front of the television
and my mother has her hand over her mouth.

Two buildings in New York City
are falling down. Matt rushes in.

"Is that a demolition?" he asks.
Mom shakes her head.

"But no one was in them," I say. "It's too early."
"It's later there," Dad says flatly, and then no one says
    anything else.

No one goes to school that day
but Mom and Dad have to go
to work so me and Matt have to go
with them. Matt says he can stay
home alone but one look from my parents
and he climbs in the car.

There are a lot of other mall brats
hanging around the mall and we come
together in groups that keep getting larger
and smaller as people wander off.
There aren't many shoppers, and everyone
has a dazed kind of zombie
look on their face.

The manager of the Gap stumbles by
and nearly bumps into the manager
of Baby Gap, who tells him he forgot to shave
the right side of his face. He puts his hands
up, *Home Alone* style, but doesn't laugh,
and normally he's a very funny guy.

Matt offers to buy me anything I want
from the food court, and promises
he won't tell Mom what I eat, but I don't think
I can get any food past the knot in my throat
that is a combination of fear
and a bunch of other things
that I can't sort out.
He presses a ten-dollar bill in my hand anyway.

Then this woman I've never seen before
comes running up to me and grabs my arm
and says, "I told you not to run
off like that!" and I can't even answer,
and Matt gets between us and says, "Hey,
back off," and the lady is like, "Oh my gosh,
I'm so sorry, I thought you were my daughter.
You're wearing the same thing."

I look down, unable to remember
what I had even put on that morning. "I'm really
sorry," she says again, before hurrying off.
We watch as her real daughter comes out
of Sharper Image and is grabbed by the arm
and then hugged.

"Let's go to the pet store," Matt suggests,
and that sounds right
so a bunch of us head down there.
We're not the only ones to have thought
of it, because Jack and Paula, the managers

of the store, have all the pets out in a big pen,
and people are on their knees petting the puppies
and snuggling with the kittens
and they are warm and soft and alive.

One of the ladies who works in the Build-A-Bear
store comes by and tells us a bloodmobile
has been set up under the skylight on the first floor.
I wish I could go build a bear right now,
but I don't want Matt to make fun of me.

We head over to find a long line of people waiting
to give blood, including one of the snobby ladies
who works at Tiffany and who once made me
wait forty-five minutes at the counter
because I'm a kid, even though I had money
from my dad to buy my mom a bracelet
for their anniversary.

A woman with a clipboard tells us
you have to be seventeen to donate,
and even though Matt is only fifteen,
he gets in line anyway and no one
questions him. I sit on the ledge of the fountain
next to Old Abe, who every year is both Santa
and the Easter Bunny, and who is also the husband
of Old Bev who works in the Information Booth.

My hand automatically reaches
into the fountain to scoop up

whatever's in reach, but I yank it out when
Old Abe jokes, "Not seventeen yet either, eh?"
My lips form the closest thing
to a smile as they've seen all day.
I shake my head.
The radio is on in the store behind us
and I can hear the announcer
talking about the damage to the Pentagon,
and saying they are close to discovering
who was responsible for this, and that
the last plane was found in Pennsylvania
and even though that is very far from here
and it wouldn't be possible,
I wonder if those passengers were flying
over my head this morning, eating peanuts
or laughing or reading or listening
to their favorite song on their Walkman.

We watch people climb into the bloodmobile
and come back out twenty minutes later
with a Band-Aid on their arm, a juice box,
and a sticker on their chest that says, "I gave today."

I turn to Abe and ask, "What do we do now?"
and I actually just meant what should we do
while Bev and Matt are in the bloodmobile,
but Abe says, "We live. In between the tragedies
is when we live." Before today I would
have thought Old Abe was just being dramatic.
Abe stands up to help Old Bev

down the bloodmobile steps and I think,
They are the reason people get married.

Matt comes out next, and his cheeks
are pale, like they took all the blood
that was in his body.

I reach into my pocket and hand
the ten-dollar bill to the lady behind the desk,
who drops it in the Red Cross donation bucket.
It occurs to me this is my first time donating anything
besides an old pair of roller skates that I had outgrown
anyway. The lady peels the back off one of the stickers
and presses it onto my chest. I wonder, vaguely,
if I will donate more things in the future.
I'd like to think so
but I don't really know.

We walk back to our mom's store and pass kids
playing on the DDR machine. We watch as they bounce
and twist and move their legs so fast they're barely visible.
And it makes me realize that all the stores
have turned off the music
that is supposed to keep
customers in the store longer.

Hearing it blast from the DDR
feels somehow disrespectful,
but it makes the lump feel a little
less there, and even though the song

is nothing more than a drumbeat
with some words that I can't even understand,
it sounds a bit like life.

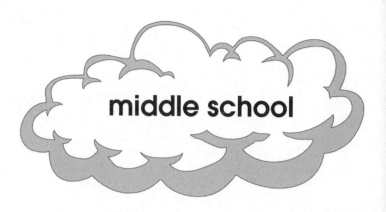
middle school

International Tobacco

Since my dad's job has something
to do with mall advertising, we get a lot
of freebies. The best was a CD Walkman
from Radio Shack, which Matt took,
so now we don't have to complain
when he blasts the Beastie Boys,
and the worst was a huge roll of cheese
from Swiss Colony which smelled really bad
and took up all this space in the fridge
until it got green and Dad threw it out.

The latest thing he got was a whole bag
of samples of a new cigarette,
which he stuck in a corner of the garage

and forgot about.
Dad quit smoking a few years ago,
not because it was bad for his health,
but because mom said the nicotine
was making his teeth brown
and no one wants to kiss an ashtray.
One day when I am home alone, I grab
a few of the packs and hide them
inside an old lunchbox that I never use,
because for a while I thought
using a lunchbox instead
of a brown paper bag would be cool,
but it never caught on at my school.

Even though Naomi is still mad
over the comment I made
about her dad being a drunk,
she wants to play with me again
simply because her mom doesn't
want her to, due to the whole
shirt-lifting incident, which still follows
me like a faithful dog.

So now Naomi is over at my house and we're
trying to think of something to do
that doesn't involve video games
or bike riding, and I remember
the cigarettes. She tells me she's never
tried smoking before, but she would

if I would. I like the idea of doing
something with Naomi that she has
never done before.

So I grab a pack of cigarettes and a box
of wooden matches, which my dad uses
to light the grill in the summers,
and we run into the woods
that line the backs of both our houses.
We sit behind a big rock
so that no one can see us and we push
the dry fall leaves away from our feet
so we don't start a fire.

It takes a few tries, but Naomi gets a match
lit, and holds it to the end of a cigarette
until it simmers and glows. Then she blows out
the match and sticks it back in the box,
which I don't think you're supposed to do,
but nothing bad happens. She hands me
the cigarette, and I put it in my mouth
and breathe in.

While I'm coughing and choking,
she takes it from my hand, puts it in her mouth,
and gently inhales. The tears in my eyes
from my stinging throat blur my vision a bit,
but not enough to miss the fact
that she is blowing perfect smoke rings.

When I've recovered enough to speak, I tell
her, "Wow, you're very good at this."
and she says, "I watch a lot of old movies."

I'm pretty sure this wasn't her first
time after all, and not wanting
to inflict further pain on my throat
or look stupid, I toss her the rest of the pack.
Her face lights up. "Thanks!" she says.
Then she reaches into the pocket
of her sweatshirt and takes out a Snickers
and presses it in my hand like a secret.

I leave her to smoke the rest of the pack,
and head back home. My parents
are still at work and Matt is at baseball practice,
so I climb out of my window and onto the roof
of the garage, where I watch Naomi
blow ring after ring, and I pull my sweatshirt tight
around me because it's brisk out.
I feel older and sort of sophisticated
even though I only took one puff
and don't plan on trying it again anytime soon.

I lean back on my elbows
and look up at the sky
and at the clouds wafting by
and I let the wind chase
the smell of smoke from my hair

and I eat my Snickers,
and the bitter taste of smoke in my mouth
almost ruins it.
Almost.

Williams-Sonoma

I can't believe I'm wearing
an apron that says "Kiss the Cook"
on it. I told my mom I needed
my own apron for cooking class,
and she said she'd bring one home
from the mall, and this
is what she comes up with?

Luckily my old enemies Jessica and Hailey
are too busy teasing my cooking partner, Amira,
because she doesn't speak English
very well, to make fun of my apron.

I want to ask Amira why she lets them
pick on her, but I'm not sure she'd

understand me, and I don't want her to
think I'm picking on her too. I used to
get frustrated when some of the people
who worked at the mall didn't speak
English very well, but then my dad asked me
how well I'd do
in any of their countries.

"Say 'I will never be loved by a man,' "
Jessica instructs Amira.
Amira repeats Jessica's words and then Jessica
and Hailey laugh and say, "Very good, you
speak very well," and Amira beams and I want
to shake her and tell her they're playing
with her but Ms. Bloomquist, the cooking teacher,
has started to come around with cups of chocolate
chips to go in the cakes we are baking. She warns
us we will only get one cup, so not to eat any of them
because they will not be replaced.

I see Amira eying the cup hungrily and I ask
if they have chocolate where she comes from.
She laughs and nods, and I think,
if she can understand what I just said,
why can't she understand Jessica and Hailey?
So when they are out of earshot, I ask her,
"Did you know that Jessica and Hailey
were just being mean to you?"

To my surprise, she nods and shrugs.
"Is easier that way," she explains.
When Jessica and Hailey go to the front
of the room to pick up their cake pans,
I quickly move over to their table
and spill their cup of chocolate chips
into the little sink. I make it back before
they notice. Amira starts laughing so hard
that snot actually comes out of her nose.

When Jessica and Hailey see what happened
they start yelling, but no one saw me do it
and Ms. Bloomquist holds firm to her threat
that the chips will not be replaced
so either they will eat them out of the sink
(which is old and moldy),
or have none at all.

The next week Amira is gone,
back to wherever she came from,
and I realize I don't even know
where that is.

Then a little package arrives in the mail
for me, which little packages never do,
and it is a chocolate bar with Hebrew
writing on the wrapper. There is no letter
or return address but I know it's from her.

It is the best present I have ever gotten.

Macy's

I've been looking forward
to the sixth-grade trip
to the Kiwanis Carnival for months,
but not because of the snow cones
and cotton candy and caramel apples
and tilt-a-whirl and carousel,
although those are great too.

I'm looking forward to it
because Andy Beckerman
will be there. He's a new kid
in my class and I happened to be
the only person in the hall
when his mother brought him in
because I didn't want to change

out of my gym clothes in front
of everyone, so I was assigned
to show him around. I kept stealing
glances at him because he's really,
really cute with green eyes
and light brown hair and a crooked smile.

For some reason, Andy believes
I am popular and told Stefanie
that he wants to ask me out. She told
him that no one "goes out"
in sixth grade, but I happen to know
he's going to ask me to ride the Ferris wheel
with him, and everyone knows
that when the Ferris wheel
gets to the top, you kiss.

Seems like a pretty good place
for a first kiss if you ask me,
especially when I know at least
three girls who would kill
to be in my sandals.

Mom gives me her Macy's card
to buy a new outfit.
It's not only that she wants me
to look good for Andy, who she knows
all about because she read a note
I had written to Stefanie,
but it's also because she feels guilty

for making me get my eyebrows
waxed last week, even though I told her
it really wasn't necessary.
Some of the skin came
off and it was a big red mess
and I couldn't go to school
for two days. Dad yelled at her
like he does whenever she tries
to improve me in some way,
and she told him he doesn't understand
what it's like being
a girl these days, and he said,
"Praise be to the gods for that!"

But instead of picking out
a new outfit, I'm planning
on getting my first bra.

I've heard all sorts of horror stories
about girls going with their mothers
to get their first bras and the old lady
in the bra department measuring them
and calling out the measurements
really loudly and there's no way
I'm going to let that happen, and in fact,
I'm not really buying a bra, so much
as I'm buying those fake rubber boobs
that you fit *inside* a bra. And I don't
need anyone calling that out, either.

I had already scoped out their location
on a previous trip, so I grab a box
and head straight to the counter.
Halfway there, I have visions
of the fake boob falling out while I walk
with a cotton candy in one hand
and a soda in the other, unable to do
anything but watch it fall in horror.
Or worse yet, I can see the headline now:
Local Girl Humiliated as Fake Boob Falls
a Hundred Feet from the Top
of the Ferris Wheel.

I replace the box on the shelf
and grab a very puffy red bra instead
and pay for it without even trying it on.

I don't have much time when I get
home, so I run up to my room
and put on my new bra. It takes
me about ten minutes to hook it
since the hook is in the back.
I slip my shirt back over my head.

Well, I'm still not *Playboy* material,
but it definitely works.

When I go downstairs
and tell my mom I'm ready for her to drive
me, I hold my jacket up in front of my chest

so she doesn't notice I have gone
through puberty overnight.

When we arrive at the carnival,
I catch up with the rest of my class
and we all go in together.
Andy and I sort of lag behind
and wind up walking next
to each other so when we all line up
at the Ferris wheel, it looks like
it is just a coincidence that we would wind
up in the same little cart,
but I know
it's not. Stefanie tries to wink at me,
but it looks like she has some sort of tick
and the teacher asks her if she's all right.

When we get in the cart,
the ride guy closes the bar and tests
that it's shut tight because last year
a girl fell from one of the rides
and got a concussion and her parents sued
for, like, a million dollars. I wonder
if it was worth it because now she's set
for life, but I heard that sometimes
she still has really bad headaches
and I think headaches are worse
than stomachaches and sore throats combined.

I start to get nervous
as our cart slowly circles its way to the top.
Andy gives me a smile, and I can tell
he's nervous too, because his lips
are quivering a bit at the corners, and his smile
is even more crooked than usual, and somehow
that makes me feel a lot better and I relax
and release the breath I have been holding.

Our cart reaches the top, and like all the others,
it pauses there for a few seconds and gently sways,
so we can see all the lights and sounds
of the carnival below. In one glance,
I see Stefanie wave up at me, a kid
in our class toss beanbags at cardboard cats,
and a little boy's cotton candy get stuck
in his sister's hair.

Andy turns to me and opens his mouth
to say something, but then he gets this weird look
on his face and turns away from me and leans
his head over the side of the cart.
I'm so busy thinking that if he doesn't kiss me
soon, our cart is going to start moving downward,
that I don't notice he has just thrown up
until I hear the person in the cart below start
screaming.

Andy turns to me and moves his head toward mine,
like he's actually going to kiss me

now, and I panic, because there's no way
I'm going to kiss someone who just threw up,
so I say, "That was some rain yesterday,"
which is a line I heard someone use in a movie
when they wanted to change the subject,
but it didn't rain yesterday,
so he just says, "Huh?" but by this time we are near
the bottom, and the kissing window has passed.

When we get off, everyone is talking
about the fact that someone threw up
on the ride, but no one knows it was Andy
and he doesn't say anything, and I don't,
and then he goes off with his friends.
I duck into the bathroom and into the one
open stall and wrestle the bra
off. I wrap it up in a ball, and toss it
in the garbage can on the way out,
where it falls amongst the soda cans,
oil-covered fried-dough plates,
and half-eaten hot dogs.

Stefanie runs over to me and asks
how the kiss was and I tell her,
"It's nothing like you see in the movies."
She says, "Bummer."
And I say, "Yeah."

Linens 'n Things

Mom and Dad are making me go
to sleepaway camp. The only other camp
I've been to was fat camp,
and that was only during the day.
Mom says it will be good for me to get a change
of scenery and says there's a special bond
between camp friends
that can last a lifetime.

I explain that I don't need more friends.
I have Stefanie and Eliza and Naomi.
But then Mom says that if I'm such good friends
with them, why don't I ever invite them
for a sleepover, and I have no answer

to that because I don't want to tell her that I'm afraid
they'll say no.

Just because Mom had, like, a million
friends when she was my age
because she competed in pageants
(a concept that makes me shiver
just thinking about it) she thinks
there's something wrong with me
because I only have three real friends,
and they each have more
important friends than me.

The only good thing about going to camp
is that I get to buy all these fun things
like tie-dyed sheets and little bottles
for shampoo and containers for soap
and slippers with bear claws at the toes
and a really soft purple bathrobe
and a cool trunk to put everything in.

As I follow my dad into the cabin
that will be mine to share with nine other girls,
I look around to see who I would want
as a lifelong friend. Should it be the two girls
rushing into each other's arms and screaming with glee?
Or the girl sitting on her bed crying
as her mom unpacks her clothes? Or maybe the girl
who is already in her full-on camp uniform?

She even used magic markers on her sneakers
to make them the yellow and blue camp colors.

Other girls come in, and they all seem to know
each other. Turns out most of the campers
have been coming here for years. They smile
at me though, and the counselor, Debbie,
gives me a warm hug and says she's soooo excited
to have me as a camper.

For the first time in my memory, I don't want my parents
to leave. One of the girls introduces herself
as Brandy, and then nudges me and says,
"Who's the hottie?" I don't need to turn around
to know she's referring to Matt, who is busy flirting
with the junior counselor.

"That would be my brother."

"You're so lucky!" she says,
pretending to swoon.
I fail to see how having a good-looking,
smart, athletic, popular brother in any way
makes me lucky, but I don't want to lose
a potential friend, so I say, "Yeah, it's great.
We hang out all the time," which is totally
not true at all.

For the first few days, having a brother
who is a hottie actually gives me a certain amount

of notoriety. When talk of the hotness
of the waterskiing instructor replaces
talk of the hotness of Matt,
I sing camp songs with a gusto
I don't really feel. I make myself laugh
really hard at the skits the counselors perform
and paint my nails blue and yellow camp colors.

No one seems to notice that I'm just going
through the motions of having camp spirit,
and they sit next to me at meals and laugh
at my jokes, because when you're overweight,
you learn to make jokes.
And maybe sometimes I'm not only going
through the motions.
It's not so bad here.
The air smells really clean and there are more stars
in the sky than I ever thought existed.
Maybe I'm like a weed
who is starting to become a flower.

The best thing is that if you don't want to swim
in the lake, you can go running on a path through
the woods instead. Since the sliminess of the lake
doesn't appeal to me, I now run each day.
It's really calming and almost feels sort of primal,
and the trees feel like they're bursting with life.
I usually have the woods all to myself
since most of the other girls
choose the lake to swim

because they can watch the water-ski instructor
as he zooms around in his power boat.

Then one day, as I should have expected,
the tide turns.
I wake up the first morning of color war,
totally unmotivated to pretend that half
of the bunk is now my enemy.
If camp is all about togetherness
and bonding, why pit half
the girls against the others?

Apparently the longtime campers take
color war very seriously, and my refusal
to run after a ball or capture a flag
has them all in a tizzy. Word around the bunk
is I'm being too nice to campers
on opposing teams and may be giving
away strategies or something.
Me – accused of being too nice.
It boggles the mind.

At dinner people make a big show
of not sitting next to me
or being my partner in anything
that requires a partner, which in camp
is a lot of things. I am not a team player,
apparently. There is no place for me here.
I am now a flower
that everyone has forgotten to water.

One day after arts and crafts, which we spent
making our initials out of wax, I return
to the bunk to find my mattress in the rafters!

Since no one will take the blame (or credit),
Debbie chooses the most likely candidates
and makes them take it down. I wind up sneezing
all night because of the dust that got on my blanket
and silently curse my parents for sending me
somewhere to become a flower and then a weed again.

The next evening the whole camp gathers
on the field to watch a movie. They hook up
a big screen and it's like a drive-in movie
without the driving part. After the movie starts,
it's easy to slip away unnoticed.

I return to the bunk and work my way down
the rows of cubbies of those on my own color
war team. Who'd have thought they'd be the ones
to turn against me?

I loosen the lid of Robin's Sea Breeze toner
and lay it on the bottom of her toiletry kit.
I take Sarah's wax initials, break them in half,
and push them back together so she won't see
the crack until she lifts them up. I slide
Ashley's retainer off the back of her cubby
until it falls down amongst the dust
and who knows what.

I move the bookmark in Claudia's book
two chapters ahead, and hide
all of Tammy's underwear in the bottom
of the bunk's dirty laundry bin.

Then I cut through the woods on the way back
to the movie site, careful to rub against
every patch of poison ivy I come across.

That night as I lie in bed itching,
I am treated to the sound of Robin
cursing at herself for leaving her Sea Breeze
unscrewed, Ashley searching everywhere
for her retainer and finally having to move
her heavy cubby to find it, Claudia musing aloud
that she doesn't understand what's happening
in her book, and Tammy finally giving up
trying to find her underwear and having to wear
her bathing suit to bed.

The next morning I am immediately sent
to the infirmary. The nurse calls my parents
and tells them I have a terrible case of poison ivy
and will have to stay in the infirmary for a week.
My father says he's not paying a thousand dollars
a week for me to lie in bed, so they come get me.

I'm so happy to see them I move in for a hug,
but they back away due to the globs
of calamine lotion covering me from head to toe.

Since my parents don't want to leave me home
alone in my condition, I have to wear long pants
and a long-sleeved shirt and go to work with them.

After using the headphones to listen to half
the new CDs at FYE, I wander through the mall
and notice something I've only glanced at before.

In the center of the mall is a tree that, each Christmas,
gets decorated and then in the summer
there are little tiny lights strewn around it.
Those things I've noticed.

But what I never noticed before is that the tree
is actually attached to the ground, with tile around it.
So the tree was here, probably
for hundreds of years, and then they must have built
the mall around it.

I put my hand against the bark and it feels
much cooler than the bark of the trees at camp,
which held the heat of the sun. I wonder
if the tree is sad that it's here instead
of in the middle of a forest.

Maybe someday I'll come to the mall early
when it's just the mall walkers out getting
their morning exercise, and the custodians
making sure we can all see the reflections of
the stores in the shiny floor,

maybe I'll come back to the tree
and cut off a branch and plant it in the woods
so that it can grow under the real sun,
and maybe a girl will run past it
and it will bring her shade.

But even as I think this,
I know I won't do it,
and that makes me sad.

The Limited Too

For every big test I've ever taken,
I wear my lucky red t-shirt
from The Limited. Actually,
I originally bought it at The Limited Too,
but I've recently outgrown their clothes.

Anyway, it has gone missing.
I can't find it anywhere in the house,
or in my gym bag, or in my parents' cars,
or in Matt's room, and today
is some big standardized test
that will determine what "track" we get
put into for the rest of middle school
and probably in high school, too.

I have no choice but to wear
a pink shirt instead. Pink is not
flattering on me, but it's the closest thing
I have to red, so on it goes. Maybe it will distract
people from the huge pimple on my chin
that has begun to cast its own shadow.

Before the test begins, my homeroom teacher
asks me to get a file for her
from the office, since my desk happens
to be closest to the door. I hurry out,
glad to have the relative freedom
that being in the hall during class provides.

When I get to the office,
I have to wait a few minutes
until the secretary can get
whatever it is my teacher needs.

I'm standing right next to the photocopy machine,
which happens to be open. Since I have nothing
better to do, I flip up the paper that is lying on the tray.
As far as I can tell, it is the answer key
to the test the whole seventh grade is about to take.

The options run through my mind.
Either I can take the paper
and hope no one misses it, or I can put
it back but press the photocopy button
and take my own copy. If I had been wearing

my red top like I should have been, I wouldn't
even need to cheat.

But if I don't do well on this test, I won't
get into college, and then I'll have to work
at the mall forever, which wouldn't be so bad
if I could work at Hollister or Sweet Delights
or FYE, so I could try on clothes, eat candy,
and listen to music all day, but knowing my luck,
I'd wind up having to work at the Vitamin Shoppe
that no one under forty goes into, or at the Hot Sam
    pretzel booth
where I'd have to wear a tall hat with a pretzel on it.

I can't take that chance.

But I can't seem to make myself
do any of the other options, either,
because then I'd have the evidence
on me, and I've seen enough television
to know you should never keep evidence
on your person.

So I stare as hard as I can at the test,
trying to memorize the pattern of answers.
I repeat them in my head,
AADCCCBBACDBABCADDB.

The secretary is heading back
into the main office, so I put the paper back

on the machine. She hands me the file,
but I'm not paying any attention
because all I'm thinking
is: *AADCCCBBACDBABCADDB.*

As I sit down to take the test with the sequence
of letters running through my head,
I am acutely aware that if I get even one wrong,
the whole pattern will be messed up,
and I'll totally bomb the test even worse
than if I didn't cheat,
and that in itself would look suspicious.

For the next week I bite my nails so far down
that they bleed. Dad asks me if I am doing it
because Mom is making me crazy
with her talk of laser hair removal for my arms,
which she thinks are getting a bit furry,
but I assure him that I have learned
to tune her out by now.

It turns out I did so well that next year
I will be in the honors classes,
and the guidance counselor calls my parents
to tell them the good news. That night
at dinner Dad raises his water glass
in a toast to me, and even Matt says something
nice, like he always knew I was smart.
Then he says he was in honors classes

when he was in middle school and he probably
still has all the homework and tests somewhere.

Dad jumps in and says, "That won't be necessary,
Matthew. Tessa has proven she is smart
enough to do just fine on her own."

After dinner I run the water in the tub really, really hot,
strip off my clothes, and climb in.
I take the loofah and vanilla bath gel
(freebies from Bath and Body Works)
and I wonder if it's possible to scrub me
off of myself.

I sink down as far as I can go,
the water whooshing into my ears,
and I lie there,
cocooned by the weight of the water
and I am a bit surprised,
although I guess I shouldn't be by now,
that this is the way the world works.

Sephora

The big thing in the beginning of eighth grade
is to pass around lip gloss
because they all have really cool flavors
that taste like real desserts but with no fat,
and the more people you share
with, the more popular you are.

I guess it was only a matter of time
until someone figured out that all this attention
to lips would lead to kissing, so when Stefanie
   (who is back
to her "fighting weight" as she calls it)
suggests we sneak out at lunch
and play spin the bottle

with some boys from our English class, I say okay.
Spin the bottle is really for kids,
but it's kind of retro, so it's cool again.

Besides me and Stefanie, there is Eliza,
who I don't see much of anymore
unless her more popular friends are busy,
and this girl Lindsey who plays the flute
in the school band and is in English with us.

The four of us
eat our soggy cafeteria pizza really fast
and then all ask for bathroom passes
from different door monitors,
only we give fake names.

The boys are already behind
the bleachers when we arrive.
Rick Vinik, who I've tried to avoid
since our fourth-grade egg incident,
Ben Silver, who is kind of punk
and whose older brother works at a store
in the mall called Against All Odds,
and Kyle Maran, a jock who reminds me
of my brother, so I hope
I don't have to kiss him.
In fact, none of them
are what I would call Prime Kissing Material,
but if I had to pick one, it would be Rick

because he has the darkest brown eyes
I've ever seen.
They are almost black.

As we sit down I ask, "Does anyone
else feel like we're in a movie
where all the bad things
happen under the bleachers?"

"Yeah," says Ben, the only person to answer.
"Sometimes I feel like my whole life
is a movie and I'm just going through the motions,
waiting for the credits at the end."

No one says anything for a minute
and I'm tempted to tell him I know
exactly what he means
when Kyle says, "If your life was a movie,
no one would pay to see it!"
This starts up a whole debate
about who would see whose movie less,
until Stefanie says, "Are we gonna get around
to the kissing, or what?" and that shuts them up.

Rick puts his mostly finished Coke can
in the middle of the circle. "I guess this
is more like spin the can," he says nervously.
The other girls and I giggle politely.
I wonder if this will be everyone's first kiss,
or just mine.

Rick leans over and spins the can around.
The opening lands on Ben. We all laugh,
and Ben puckers up. This gets us laughing
harder. "You wish," Rick says, and spins
again. This time it lands on Eliza.
I'm a little disappointed.

Eliza hesitates for a second, and then tucks
her shiny-as-ever hair behind her ears and leans forward.
Rick leans in toward her, and they meet
in the middle with their lips. I've never seen
anyone kiss that close up before, not even my parents.

We all cheer. Eliza spins and it lands
back on her. She kisses her hand
and we laugh again. I feel very close
to these people right now. She spins
again and gets Ben. Without hesitating
this time, she scoots forward and plants
a kiss on him before
he even has a chance to prepare.

Ben spins now, and it seems like the can
is going around forever
before it finally lands halfway between
me and Lindsey.

"Who's it gonna be?" Kyle asks.
Ben looks startled, like he didn't
expect to be in this situation.

I hope he doesn't pick me.
I just don't understand the whole
punk thing. Why would someone
want to like the same bands
his parents did?

"Tessa," he says softly.
My heart quickens a little,
and I think how the only thing
I've ever said to Ben before this
was "Do you have a piece of gum?"
after I had garlic at lunch
and I saw him chewing gum in the hall.
Not exactly the witty banter I imagined
would precede my first kiss.

I don't move for a second, and the girls
start chanting my name. "Tess-a! Tess-a!"
I take a deep breath and lean forward.
Ben's lips touch mine, and I close my eyes.
Time seems to slow down
and all I can feel is his lips,
not even the ground I'm sitting on.
We must have stayed like that for a while,
because the boys are hooting now.

The bell rings for the end of lunch,
so Kyle kisses both Lindsey and Stefanie.
We all race in different directions
to our next class.

As I run, I whip out
my cheesecake-flavored lip gloss
and roll it over my lips again and again,
sealing in the kiss.

Abercrombie & Fitch

I'm not saying that I want to be a prep.
It's just that by the end of eighth grade
my chest is finally big enough
(not big, just big enough) and I've lost
enough weight due to the treadmill
Mom bought me for Christmas
(even though I asked for an iPod
and I told her I could run for free
if I wanted to, but I haven't been able
to make myself do it after that whole
camp fiasco), but anyway I am now able
to wear one of those tight tank tops
and I really want to try one.

So one afternoon I make my first trip
into Abercrombie & Fitch with the intention
to buy something. I've only browsed
before, in awe that people could actually
be small enough to fit in these clothes.
As I cross under the sign, I can't help
but wonder how poor Fitch feels,
since everyone calls the store Abercrombie,
and I make a mental note that if I ever have a partner
in something, I have to make sure
to put my name first.

I pick out a few different styles
and ignore the raised eyebrows of the clerk
when I ask her to open a dressing room.

The first one flattens out my boobs
under a built-in bra. That's no good.
The next pushes them up so high
it's like they're twice their size. From the neck down,
I don't recognize myself. I feel detached,
like what it must be like when you die
and look down and see your body
and you think it must be someone
else's body, except I'm not dead,
I'm just in a push-up tank top.

I buy it in turquoise because I read
in *Seventeen* that turquoise looks good
on everyone.

When I walk downstairs to breakfast
my dad points to the stairs and says, "March,"
but it's actually May so I'm confused.

"Back up and change," he says.
"You're not wearing that."

"It's just a shirt from the mall," I argue.
"Everyone wears them." He keeps pointing,
no longer looking up from his cereal bowl.

With a loud sigh, I go back upstairs and throw
a sweatshirt on over the tank. I go back down.
"Happy now?" I ask. "Exceedingly," he replies,
giving me a quick glance. A small part of me
is disappointed by his inability to recognize
what must be a common teenage ploy.

I run into Stefanie as I get off the bus and she asks,
"Aren't you hot in that?" I nod, pull the sweatshirt off,
and tie it around my waist. Her eyes widen a bit
when she sees my shirt, but she doesn't say anything.
That's one of the cool things about Stefanie.
As my oldest friend, she doesn't judge.

All down the hall kids stare at me. Boys and girls
alike. At first I think it's fun and I stand up taller.
Then the vice principal walks by and when he passes
me, he cranes his head around to stare a little longer
and he almost bumps into these two kids making out

against a locker and he gives them both detentions
for public display of affection.

I have to stop in the library to return an overdue book,
and two preps are in there using the computer.
They look up when I walk in, and their eyes take in
my outfit from head to toe.

I hold my breath, and they both give little head nods
of approval. Excellent!

About halfway through social studies, an office aide
comes into our room and hands my teacher, Mr. Meyer,
a note. He reads it, and motions to me. I turn to look
behind me, because why would that note be about me?
I do a quick scan of my memories to see if I did anything
recently that might warrant such attention.
Nothing comes to mind.

Is it my imagination, or does the whole class watch me
leave the room with slightly more intensity
than they otherwise would have?

"Where are we going?" I ask the aide.

"Vice principal's office," she replies.

Once again, I scan my brain. Forge late slips?
Not in weeks. Cut gym class? Not since last month
when I had my period and there was no way

I was going to climb ropes. Cheated?
Not since last week when I let Barry Villano copy
my math answers, and in that case
it was really he who was cheating, not me.

"Why am I going to the vice principal's office?
Is it because of that overdue book? I know
it was really overdue, but these honors classes
make you do all this outside reading
and it just took me longer than I thought."

The aide looks at me as if I'm stupid and says,
"It's not your overdue book."

"What, then?"

"Well, your outfit might have something to do with it."

"My outfit?" I repeat. But her lips are sealed
in a straight line now. She opens the door for me
and points to a chair outside the office. This is
the first time I've sat in this chair without knowing
what I did to get here. With middle school
almost at its end, I had hoped to glide
through the rest of it. Not to be, apparently.

The VP opens his door and waves me in.
"I only have a second, Miss Reynolds. If you don't
have something more appropriate to put on,
I'm going to have to send you home for the day."

I don't know how to respond to this,
so I don't say anything.

He continues. "Your outfit does not comply
with the school's dress code."

"We have a dress code?"

"We do indeed. And your tank top violates it.
Do you, or do you not, have a suitable replacement?"

I hesitate. I hear my dad's voice in my head saying,
"Choose your battles." Do I really want to choose this
    one?
I tell him I have a sweatshirt in my backpack,
and pull it out to show him.

He nods. "That will be fine. We usually send a note
home to the parents when this happens,
but since you are willing to rectify
the situation, I'm going to let it go."

Well, there's that at least. Dad doesn't have to know.
I slip the sweatshirt over my head, feeling a bit
like I'm getting dressed in front of a stranger.

So this whole thing didn't work out
the way I planned. I should have listened to Dad
and worn something less problematic. Of course
that would involve listening to Dad.

I refuse to go back to class in my sweatshirt,
so I go into the bathroom to hide. A goth girl
is standing an inch away from the mirror. Her hand
is covering her face, but I can tell she's crying.

"Are you okay?" I ask, slightly surprised
that someone else could be having a crappy day.

She nods. "I'm just piercing my nose. Hurts a little."

"Ahh. Good luck with that." I turn around before I see
blood and lock myself in the last stall. But after a minute
it occurs to me that it really smells, and if I linger in here
too long, the smell will stick to me.

I leave the stall, and thankfully all that is left of the goth
    girl
is a bloodstained paper towel on the sink. I stand in front
of the full-length mirror at the end of the bathroom.
I wonder if the boys' room has a full-length mirror.
I bet not.

I take off the sweatshirt and try to see myself
as others do. I honestly don't remember it being this
    low-cut
in the store. But I don't think it's that big a deal.
Don't these people watch MTV? Those girls
show a lot more flesh than this.

Okay, so maybe you can see more
of my boobs than is perhaps appropriate for school.
But I think I look good. Not skinny, but still good,
and I never think I look good.

A girl named Cassandra comes in. She's the queen
of the preps and an Abercrombie regular. I consider
ducking back in a stall, but it's too late. She fixes
her makeup in the mirror, washes her hands,
says, "Your tank's on backwards," and leaves.

high school

Old Navy

I.

Lucas. Lucas of the long brown hair
that he's always pushing away from
the bluest eyes I've ever seen on a boy.
Lucas of the white teeth and warm smile.
He's worked in Old Navy
for three weeks, three days, and three hours.
All those threes must mean something.
I think they mean I'm supposed to go
over there today and profess my love.

I know I'm a freshman and he's a junior,
but it's only the beginning of the year

and I can pretend I don't know the rules
about who can pursue who.

But I did grow two inches over the summer
so my curves have fallen
into better positions than they were before.
Or at least that's what Stefanie told me.
Plus, I think Lucas likes me. Why else
would he have brought me right over
to where the flip-flops were, instead
of just pointing, which he totally could have
done because they weren't that far away.

And then a few days later, he was buying
a paperback copy of *The Road Less Traveled*
at Brentano's, and I was there waiting
for my mother to drive me home, and he asked
my name and then he said he'd never heard it
before and that it was really pretty.
Then he asked if my parents named me Tessa
after the Tesseract in that kids' book
A Wrinkle in Time
and wasn't that such a great book?

I almost said it was more likely
my mom would have named me
Chanel or Estée Lauder or Clinique
than a character from a book but I just shook
my head and said, "They named me
after my dad's favorite aunt, who used

to make him lemonade with real sugar cubes."
And then I spent the next hour berating
myself for adding the part about the sugar cubes,
which must have sounded really weird.

In the past three weeks I've bought six t-shirts from him
in assorted colors, the aforementioned flip-flops,
a tiny notebook with Hello Kitty on the cover,
a pair of tan capris with flowers down one leg,
and a 3-pack of underwear
that is a size too small for me, but I want him
to think that's the size I wear.

And each time I go in there, he says,
"Hi, Tesseract," and smiles at me, and not
in that phony salesman kind of way. A real smile.
After all my time in the mall, I way know the difference.

II.

Today's the day. All those threes. Eliza has offered
to help me because she's a big believer in fate
and taking matters in your own hands.
This would seem to be contradictory,
but really it isn't. She has to bring her little sister
Samantha, who is almost five and has this habit
of asking strangers for hugs. Eliza's parents tried
keeping her on one of those leashes,
but she actually bit through it.

Our first stop is Bath & Body Works, where we smear
grapefruit-pineapple-apple moisturizer all over
my arms and legs, because Eliza read in *Seventeen*
that the smell of citrus makes people happy.

Then we head up to Sephora to "sample" the makeup,
which is much more fun than my mother's boring
    makeup.
Eliza lines my eyes with a smudgy black eyeliner to make
them look smoky and mysterious, and then just for fun,
she adds a Harry Potter scar in the middle
of my forehead, and little antlers on Samantha's.

To get her back, I draw a heart on her cheek
with ruby red lipstick. I scrub off the lightning scar,
but she leaves the heart.

We head over to the hair-care section, where one drop
of this really expensive smoothing serum makes
all my flyaways lie flat. If I worked at the mall,
I would do all my grooming here for free.

Meanwhile Samantha has asked for, and received,
hugs from an old lady buying bath beads
in Bath & Body Works, a woman pushing a stroller
on the way to Sephora, and Old Abe.

I feel ready to talk to Lucas now, but Eliza says I need
sustenance first, so we head over to the food court,

where we load up on samples of Kung Pao Chicken,
shot-glass portions of strawberry-banana smoothies,
and tiny chunks of Cinnabons. Mmmm . . . Cinnabons!
The world's most perfect food.

Eliza walks me to Old Navy. Before I go in,
I ask her, "Do I have anything in my teeth?"
and she says, "Just teeth."

"Wish me luck," I say, smoothing down
my miniskirt. Samantha gives me a big bear hug
and I have to detach myself before her sticky fingers
get all over my clothes. Eliza says,
"You won't need luck in that skirt!"

It really is a cool skirt. It has three layers of ruffles
and not much else. Dad would hate it. Luckily he's out
of town on business, spying on other malls.

Maybe my mother is right —
when you look good, you feel good,
and I know I look good, but it's
fat-girl-good, which is different.
I take a deep breath, head inside the store,
and at first I don't see him.
Could I have gotten his hours wrong?
I've been carefully charting them since he started.

And then I see him. Lucas of the broad shoulders.
I'm about to peer around the other side

of those shoulders, when I catch a glimpse
of someone already there.
Someone with long blond hair in a high ponytail,
the kind no one wears anymore unless
they are running across a field somewhere
with a stick or a ball. They are standing close
and whispering, and I think I recognize her
as one of the girls who works at J.Crew.

My heart sinks. It feels like it actually drops
a little in my chest. All this preparation for
nothing. All this buildup in my head.
I should have known better than to think a guy
like Lucas would like me.

But wait. What if she is his sister?
Maybe she's telling him that their father
said to come straight home after work because
the whole family is going out to celebrate
her being chosen for the field hockey team.

He says something that I can't hear,
and then she reaches up and kisses him
on the lips.

Crap! Oops, I might have said that out loud,
because they both turn to look at me.

"Hi, Tesseract!" says Lucas of the searing blue eyes.
I smile weakly and pretend to be interested
in the selection of sun visors with stupid sayings on them.

To the sister-no-more, he says, "Tessa
was named after a book. Isn't that cool?"

I don't bother to correct him
because he just said my name
and the word "cool"
in the same sentence.

The girl narrows her eyes at me, but says,
"Yeah, that's really cool."

Then he says he has to get back to work,
and she kisses him again, longer than I think
is necessary, and turns to go.

As she passes by me, she looks my outfit up
and down and whispers,
"You have food in your teeth."

My first reaction is to run my tongue over
my teeth in a panic, but then I remember
that I already passed the teeth-check from Eliza.

I watch her sashay out of the store, swinging
her pocketbook, and I think, well,
she started it.

III.

"So what can I help you with today?" Lucas asks.

"Is that your girlfriend?"

He nods. "Three months now."

"She works in J.Crew, right?"

"Yup." He picks up a shirt someone had left
on the wrong table and begins folding it.

"Well, last week I saw her making out with that guy
who works at Spencer's with all the tattoos
and the earring in his eyebrow."

He stops in mid-fold. "Are you sure?"

I nod, remembering the old adage,
If you're going to lie, be specific. So I say,
"I saw them in a corner booth at Johnny Rockets.
They were sharing a huge pile of french fries
and they were really going at it."

His eyes get a little glassy, and I instantly feel bad.
Who knew he was so sensitive?

"Hey, look," I tell him. "I'm really sorry.
Maybe it wasn't her."

He shakes his head. "No, it probably was.
The other night she brought over this game
from Spencer's, you know, one of those,
well, you're too young, so never mind."

"Hey, everything I learned about sex,
I learned from Spencer's."

"Everything?" he teases.

Since I don't think my one foray
into spin the can counts, I change the subject.
"I have two passes to the movies upstairs,
if you wanna go. You get off soon, right?"

I want to bite my tongue
as soon as the words come out,
but he smiles and says, "Yeah,
in about half an hour. Meet you then?"

I wander around the store picking things up,
putting them down, not seeing anything,
just hearing my heart pound. We have a date!

He leads me on a roundabout route
to the theater, and I know he's doing it
so we don't pass J.Crew, but I don't care.
He asks if I'm going to want any popcorn
or candy so that he can stop at the mall ATM first,

and even though I would love some popcorn or candy,
I tell him I won't.

"What movie do you want to see?"
he asks as we join the few other people
who have chosen a movie in the middle
of the day. I used to wonder who those people were,
and now I am one of them.

"Surprise me," I reply.

So of course he picks something with car chases
and banter between mismatched partners,
but I don't even mind because he has just taken
my hand and the lights have just dimmed.

Although admittedly, his hand is really clammy.
Like, dead-fish clammy. And sticky.
Stickier than Samantha's.

A kissing scene comes on the screen and he turns
to me and whispers, "You know, I think you're really cool.
And not just because you're named after the Tesseract."

"What exactly IS a Tesseract?" I whisper back.

He raises his brows in surprise.
Had he really expected me to know this?

"A Tesseract is a kind of web that takes you
from one place in space to another one really far away,
without going through all the stuff in between."

While I search my brain for some response to that,
he turns my head toward him and before I know it,
we're kissing. Like, really kissing. With tongues.

Is it supposed to be this wet? This, er, awkward?
Am I supposed to taste what he had for lunch?
My one kiss with Ben was a lot better.
Would it be rude of me to pull away?

Fortunately I don't need to find out
because the usher shines a flashlight right in our faces
and we pull apart.
I make a mental note to thank him later.

Lucas continues to hold my hand, though.
There is now actual liquid squished between
his hand and mine. Doesn't he feel it?

Will this movie EVER END?

IV.

Lucas is apparently one of those people who sits
through every movie credit, so I take the opportunity

to go to the bathroom and clean off my hands.
What I wouldn't give for a mint to rid me
of the lingering taste of his bean burrito.

After the movie we pass the arcade and he says,
"I just have to do one thing, okay?
I'm about to get the top score on Aliens Attack."

I say, "Sure," because as long as he's playing
a video game, he can't hold my hand.
An hour and twenty minutes later, it dawns on me
that I must be the lamest person on earth
to still be standing here watching this guy
shoot aliens who actually don't seem like they'd do any
   harm
if they landed on earth.

So I leave.

I'd like to say he runs out after me, but he doesn't
even take his hands off the laser guns.

When I get home I call Eliza
and fill her in on the kiss.
She says yes, it's supposed to be wet,
and no, I'm not supposed to be able
to tell that his last meal was at Taco Bell.

She promises it will get better
but I tell her I think the whole

French-kissing thing is overrated
and she laughs and says I need
to find better partners, preferably those
who don't already have girlfriends.

I want to tell her that it's easy for her,
but I can't be so picky. Guys who want
to kiss me don't come along every day.
I don't say that though, because I know
she wouldn't understand.

All I can do is hope that the next guy
has Cinnebon for lunch instead.

Supply Closet

I.

In bio sophomore year I get put
in a study group with two jocks
and a cheerleader.
I debate asking the teacher
to let me switch, but I don't want
to cause trouble because I'm already facing
a B-, and these three seem pretty smart.

The cheerleader is named Sloane.
She is the token size 12
on the squad, so we should get
along pretty well.

The jocks are both named Dave,
so we decide to call them Big Dave
and Little Dave, and Little Dave
isn't even insulted because they are both huge,
it's just that Big Dave has bigger teeth.
That boy's teeth are really quite large.

Maybe it's because we know
we'll never hang out after this,
or maybe because after dissecting an earthworm
together we feel unnaturally close,
but for some reason we start telling each other
things that we never told anyone before.

I know that Little Dave still sleeps
with a stuffed frog named Jumpers, that Big Dave
knows all the words to the *Grease* soundtrack,
and that Sloane was on the news
when she was six months old
because her dad was supposed to drop her
off at daycare, but forgot
she was in the car and went to work.
By the time he remembered, the police had already
    rescued Sloane,
who was still asleep in her car seat.

The only thing I told them about me
was that one time I peed standing up
to see what it felt like.

After our final meeting, the Daves suggest
we toilet-paper this guy's house
who is the quarterback
at our rival high school.

In-class friends aren't supposed
to do anything social out of school,
that's why they're called in-class
friends. And in-class friends
are even a step below in-*school*
friends, which would mean we'd be friends
in any class we were in together.
Even though we've shared secrets,
The four of us are definitely in-class
friends who are now in
uncharted territory.

And TP-ing someone's house
sounds very stupid,
but when was the last time
two jocks and a cheerleader
asked me to do anything?

So after dinner that night we meet
at the Quick Check. Sloane grabs
a few packs of toilet paper,
but when she goes to pay for them,
the guy behind the desk tells her
that teenagers can only buy one
four-pack per day.

"But what if I have, you know,
serious bathroom problems?"

"Do you?" he asks, "have serious
bathroom problems?"

Little Dave says, "Oh, you should hear
the things that come out of her."
The guy shakes his head. "Sorry.
I don't make the rules."

So this is what the popular kids do
when they get together? Should I just leave?
Then Big Dave puts his arm around me
and says, "I'm glad you came;
you won't be sorry." And suddenly I am
glad I came. What else would I be doing?
Watching *American Idol*?

"I know where we can get as much toilet paper
as we need," I hear myself announce.

We squeeze into Little Dave's car
(which he's not really supposed to be driving
because he only has his permit)
and drive to the mall.

I lead them in through an employee entrance,
which happens to be right across
from the enormous supply closet,

which I happen to have a key for. Voilà!
All the toilet paper one could ever want.
I've never broken in here before,
although since I used a key, it's not exactly breaking in.
This place was always hallowed ground –
where Dad would take me when I was little
to marvel at all the neat rows
of toilet paper, boxes of plastic silverware,
paper towels, staplers, hangers. Everything.
And now I am ruining those perfect rows,
that perfect symmetry
of Stuff.

I guess this *is* what the popular kids do.

We shove as much as we can fit
under our jackets and run back outside.
Little Dave drives us to the next town over.
He parks the car a few houses away,
and quickly turns off the headlights.
Big Dave has already instructed us
on proper procedure. We are each to stand
under a tree, and toss the roll
as high as we can, and then try to catch it
on the way down so it doesn't get all wet
by hitting the ground.

It is dark and quiet,
and I can hear crickets

and someone's television
tuned to *American Idol*.

We run to the boy's yard,
and each take position
under a different tree. Big Dave counts
down on his fingers, and when he gets to one,
we toss our rolls with all our might
so they go over the branches.

I'm struck by how beautiful
it is. All these streams of white
paper float through the air
like silent fireworks.

We repeat this over and over
until the whole yard
is dripping in white.

I don't know why people
would complain about this
when it's obviously a work of art.

And it's not only the beauty
of it, the whole thing is very freeing.
Just tossing the paper
with abandon.

One of the Daves lets out a "Whoop!"
and I totally understand how he feels.

But then the lights go on in the house,
and Big Dave yells, "Run!"

II.

Sloane and I run in one direction,
and the Daves in another.
For a larger girl, Sloane sure can run.
I follow her back onto the main road,
where she ducks inside Walmart.
I've never actually been inside a Walmart
before. Being a mall brat,
it's very frowned upon to shop elsewhere.
I had no idea they had so much stuff.
It will be easy to blend in here,
in case we were followed.

"C'mon," Sloane says, yanking me
to the hat section. She throws a floppy pink hat
on my head and puts a straw one on her own.

"Um, this might make it harder
to blend in, don't you think?"

She shakes her head. "I've learned
that the more you look different
from everyone else, the less people actually notice
you. It's like their eyes just gloss right over you."
I'm about to tell her that's ridiculous,

but then I actually think about it.
Like when I see someone in a wheelchair
I sort of look around them
instead of directly at them,
because I don't want them to think
I'm staring at them, but maybe it's even worse
to pretend they're not there in the first place.

By this point it's clear
no one is chasing after us.
Sloane calls one of the senior cheerleaders
to come get us, since we obviously can't
go back to Dave's car, or even risk
calling him on his cell phone.

When Sloane's friend arrives
I see she brought two other girls,
so it's a tight fit, but I feel important
and cool. I'm hanging out
with the cheerleaders,
and they're the coolest girls in school.

Plus we both forgot
to take our hats off
so that's kind of funny,
although I guess it's shoplifting
even if we didn't mean to take them.

Of course, it would be better
if someone actually said something

to me other than to ask where I live
so they can drop me off.
Sloane didn't even introduce me
when we got in. In case they're not talking
to me because of the hat, I take it off
and put it on my lap.

They pull up in front of my house,
and as I'm getting out,
one of the girls says, "Nice shoes!
Where'd you get them, Walmart?"
and the rest of them laugh,
even Sloane, which makes me wish
I hadn't told her about the peeing-standing-up thing.

I look down at my feet.
I love my pink high-tops.
I bet they think I'll throw them out now.

Instead, I wear them every day
for the rest of the week,
and THEN I throw them out,
which is a totally different thing.

Mrs. Fields

After the incident where Matt ruined
my mother's leftover birthday cake
I haven't wanted cake
for my birthday, because every time I eat
a piece, it tastes like mustard.

So even though Matt is away
at college and my birthday cake
would be guaranteed mustard-free,
my mom picks up one of those
huge cookies from Mrs. Fields
that says *Happy Sweet Sixteen*
in different-color icing,
because you can't put mustard
inside a cookie.

I look forward to my birthday
every year because it is the only time
Mom gives me real desserts
instead of healthy things
like soy and rice milk dressed up
to look like chocolate pudding
and whipped cream.

We're going to eat the big cookie tonight
when Stefanie, Eliza, and Naomi
come for a sleepover.

I think we're supposed to
paint each other's toenails,
tell secrets,
dance in our underwear,
and have pillow fights
(unless that's just in the movies),
but I really wouldn't know
because this will be my first one.
I think I'm mostly doing it
to prove to my mother
that my friends will come.

Eliza almost has to cancel
to babysit her sister,
but she hires a neighbor to do it,
which proves to me
how much she wants to be here
for my birthday.

Naomi doesn't know Eliza and Stef
very well, since she's older,
but she and Eliza hit it off right
away, because they are both cool.

After we eat the cookie,
Eliza and Naomi compare bands
that I've never heard of,
and Stefanie slips into the bathroom
and I hear some sounds
that make me think
I should go in there to see
if she's okay, but even though Stef and I
have always struggled with our weight,
we don't talk about the kinds of things
that might be behind
her making those noises,
and I assume that her sister
would have said something to her
if there was a problem.

So instead, I turn the music up louder
so Eliza and Naomi don't hear.

Later that night Naomi decides
we should play
truth or dare.

She says she'll start, so Eliza asks her,
"Truth or dare."

"Dare," she says,
because that's the kind of girl she is.

Eliza dares her to run around
the block in just her bra
(and it's a REALLY long block),
and she does it! And her bra
isn't even one of those
nice ones – it's kind of ratty,
like she certainly didn't expect anyone to see it.
We run behind her, cheering her on
and laughing. A car drives by and honks.
Naomi waves, and I think, *This is what a sleepover
party is supposed to be.*

Back up in the room, it's Eliza's turn,
and I ask her, "Truth or dare?"

"Truth," she says,
because that's the kind of girl she is.

Before I can change my mind
I ask, "What do you like least
about me?" I hold my breath
for her answer.

Eliza may be beautiful
and popular but she is honest,
and I know she'll tell me the truth.

"Sometimes," Eliza says,
not meeting my eyes, "it feels
like you're always around. At school,
I mean. Like if I turn around,
you're there."

Her words seem to flatten
out the air in the room,
and when I inhale
it feels like nothing comes in.

No one looks at anyone.

My mother knocks on the door
and then sticks her head in.
"Time for cake," she says,
then corrects herself.
"I mean, time for cookie."

On the way downstairs,
Eliza says, "Forget I said anything,
it was stupid. It was just the game."

I nod and say no problem,
but I know it's not just the game.
It's not like I follow Eliza around.
It's not like I worship her or anything.

Maybe I just take up more space
than some other people, and that's why
she sees me a lot.

Later, after the cookie
and soda and awkward birthday singing,
no one wants to play the game
anymore. I'm disappointed.
I would have chosen dare,
because that's the kind of girl I am.

Gift Cards Aplenty

Since apparently your junior year
is your last chance to look good
on college applications,
my parents are making me
join an after-school activity
this year.

I've never paid much attention
to the clubs at school
since I'm not really much
of a joiner. I pick up a list
in the guidance office.
The choices are vast.
A lot of people must be concerned
about getting into college,

because there are clubs
for: chess, art, computers,
photography, movie-making,
movie-watching, debate, mathletes,
Amnesty International, yearbook,
the literary magazine, manga,
science, local activism, philosophy,
G.L.A.D, bowling, newspaper,
skiing, drama, student government,
anime, biking, modern dance, choir,
Greenpeace, Habitat for Humanity,
knitting, creative writing, car repair,
robotics, S.A.D.D., and, yes, juggling.

I've always wanted to learn to juggle,
but somehow I don't think
that's what my parents have in mind.

Eliza is in debate, modern dance,
and on the yearbook committee.
I don't think any of those are right for me,
and after the things she said
at my sleepover party, I've been good
at keeping my distance at school,
even though she makes a big show
of being very friendly when she sees me
in the hall.

I figure the drama club might be a good fit
because when I cried for two days

because my parents wouldn't let me
have a computer in my room,
Mom called me a drama queen.

Plus, when I was little,
I used to pretend I was Maria
in *The Sound of Music*.

I've never even spoken
to any of the drama kids before,
but when I turn up at the first meeting
I see that the drama isn't just on the stage.
The guys are very emo,
and the girls are a mix of goth and scene,
and I don't really understand what the whole scene
thing is about or why teenage girls would want to wear
little bows in their hair like they are five,
but I think it's something about music.

I quickly realize that these aren't the kids
who put on the school plays like *Guys and Dolls*,
Oklahoma, or anything old-fashioned like that.
These are the kids who perform one-man shows
about death and despair and being alone
in a world that doesn't understand you.
I don't know if I have enough black
in my wardrobe to fit in here.

They're having some sort of debate
about whether or not it is possible

to believe in anything outside of yourself.
Have I wandered into the philosophy club
by mistake?

I figure if I don't say anything,
maybe they'll assign me something
like painting a set, which would probably be easy
because all I would need
is black paint.

But I guess I stand out too much in my red
cami and capris, and one of the girls –
who for some reason is wearing a scarf
when it's still over seventy degrees outside –
says, "Hey, New Kid, are you a solipsist?"

"Huh?" I ask, hoping that it's nothing
bad or fatal. "A solipsist," she repeats,
"is someone who thinks that they are
the only thing that really exists.
Everything else is in their imagination."

The twelve or so others have turned my way,
waiting for a response. "Um, no, I'm pretty sure
other things exist besides me."

"But are you SURE?"
a boy with heavy black eyeliner asks.

"Well, if I pinch you and you scream,
will that be proof enough?"

A few people laugh, and the boy smiles,
but shakes his head. "All it would prove
is that in your imagination, I screamed."

I am not sure where this conversation
is going to go, and I'm worried
that saying I believe in things
other than my own existence has threatened
the possibility of them accepting me.
So I go with the only option left to me:
"Does anyone want some beer?"

We happen to have cases and cases of beer
piled up in the garage, because the guy who opened
the gift certificate kiosk at the mall once gave my dad
a one-year subscription to the beer-of-the-month club,
but for some reason it just keeps coming.
It's going on six years now.

"I like your style, New Girl,"
the boy with the eyeliner says. So we pile
into three cars and head to my house,
where a few people get out and help
me move some of the beer from the back
of the pile into the trunks of the cars,
and then we drive to one girl's house
who lives in the hills and must be really rich

because a lot of the house is made of glass
and she has a huge pool with two hot tubs
and no visible parents.

To my surprise, the girls strip down
to their underwear, and the boys take
off their black jeans before climbing
into one of the two hot tubs. I don't think
this is the first time they've come here after school.

One guy opens beer after beer with his teeth,
which doesn't seem like a smart idea,
but he doesn't need me to tell him that.

It's not my first beer ever, but it's the first
one I actually finish. I take off my flip-flops
and sit on the edge of the hot tub. There is no way
I'm going to show everyone my underwear
an hour after meeting them.

The conversation goes back and forth between
whether trying to capture life on a stage
can ever truly portray it accurately,
to whether the era of the big-breasted pop star is over.

After an hour it occurs to me
that I don't know anyone's name,
not even the girl whose house this is,
and I'm starting to feel

like I don't want to be here anymore.
Everyone is talking
but no one is listening
except for me,
because I've never been around
so many people who have so much to say
and I'm starting to wonder
if something is wrong with me,
because I can't think of a single thing
I want to tell them,
so I tell Eyeliner Boy
that I have to get home for dinner,
and he says he'll take me, no problem.

Everyone waves and says thanks for the beer,
and its obvious it's the beer
they wanted to hang out with, not me.
But it's nice to be popular even for an hour.

In the car he talks about how he wants
to be an actor after graduation, but a stage
actor, not a movie actor, since acting
in movies isn't even real because you just say
a few lines and they keep stopping
to shoot other angles so it's like being
a trained pony. Eyeliner Boy is not afraid
to say what he thinks. I wonder
what my parents would think if they saw me
in a car with a guy wearing makeup.

We pull up in front of my house,
and I am ready to hop out
when he says, "Here, you might want this,"
and hands me a breath mint.

"Right," I say. "Forgot about the beer breath."

He shakes his head. "No, I thought
you might want to kiss me."

This snaps me out of my daydream
of Mom asking Eyeliner Boy
where he gets his makeup, in the hopes
of getting me interested in wearing more.

I honestly hadn't considered kissing him,
but I think I'm ready to try again
and at least I know
he has fresh breath.
He leans over, and I smell the peppermint
before his lips reach mine.

Soon we are full-on kissing
and he is much better than Lucas
from Old Navy. I'm hoping
I'm doing it right, when he pulls away
and says, "Hmm, that's not how it is
with Brittany."

"Huh?" I say, confused.

"Brittany," he repeats. "My girlfriend.
The one in the scarf?"

"Huh?" I say again.

"Yeah," he says. "With her it's like I can feel
myself alive in her mouth,
like I'm the life force itself,
and she's like this beam of energy and –"

I cut him off by getting out of the car
and closing the door. I bet
the kids in the juggling club
don't wonder if they're the only thing
that exists in the world.
Although now that I think of it,
if I was the only real thing
God would probably call a do-over.

Oshman's Sporting Goods

I.

Mom and Dad have decided
it's time we take a family vacation.
We've never taken one before
since holidays are such a busy time
at the mall and my parents usually can't
get away.

But after sixteen years,
they've finally decided
the mall can get along without them
for one Thanksgiving,

so we're going skiing,
and we're going on an airplane.

I've never been skiing,
and I've never been on an airplane.
I don't know which one
freaks me out more.

All four of us go to Oshman's
to get outfitted in ski attire,
from head to toe. I feel like
I should be in an ad, standing
on a mountaintop, a cold drink
in my hand.

Eliza tells me for luck,
I have to touch the outside of the plane and Stefanie
gives me a whole box of gum,
because she says you have to keep
chewing or else your eardrums will burst.

Naomi warns me not to sit
next to any cute guys on the plane,
because a lot of people traveling
on business take off their wedding rings.
Somehow I don't think
that will be an issue for me.

Matt hasn't flown before either,
but he's pretending he's not nervous

by spouting off all these statistics
about the safety of air travel,
which just shows that he actually looked
up those statistics in the first place.

As we board the plane I follow
Eliza's instructions and lay my hand
flat against the cool hull of the plane.
Armed with my box of gum and the iPod
I finally got for my birthday, I settle
into my window seat with Matt on the aisle
and an empty seat between us.
Mom and Dad are a few rows ahead of us
with their heads bent close to each other.
From here it looks like they're laughing,
which is a nice change. Not that they fight
a lot – they just don't normally do
much of anything.

Matt fastens his seat belt
and closes his eyes. Mine are wide
open. I read the safety card twice, study
the instructions on the barf bag
(pretty much just aim and fire away), and watch
the metal flaps sticking out of the wings
as they go up and down like a bird
preparing for flight.

When the plane actually starts moving,
I grip the armrests and notice Matt is doing

the same thing. The nose of the plane lifts off
the ground, and it doesn't seem like we're going
fast enough for it to be able to do that,
but now the back wheels are off the ground
and this huge mammoth metal beast is flying
into the clouds.

I knew that objects on the ground would
look tiny, but I had no idea how orderly
everything would be. Nice even grids
of houses and towns and fields. I drag myself
away from the window only to eat
the bag of roasted nuts
the flight attendant hands me.

At one point the captain comes on to say
we're about to run into some mild turbulence,
and I can see Matt's shoulders tense up,
but all it feels like to me is a bumpy road.

The flight is short, and in an hour
we are touching down and there is snow
on the ground. Matt finally opens his eyes.

"You missed the whole thing," I tell him.
He just grunts. On the way down the aisle
I pass the little nook where the flight attendants
make the food for first class, and a whole plate of cookies
is just sitting there, so I take one and then one more,

because it's not like they could reuse them
on the next trip, I don't think.

The pilot of the plane is still in the cockpit,
and I want to thank him for the flight,
because I bet not a lot of people do that,
but my mouth is too full of chocolate chip cookie,
and I don't want to spray his uniform.

II.

The skiing portion of the trip
doesn't go as well for me as the flight.
I just cannot manage to balance
on two slippery slabs of metal
or plastic or whatever they are.
The rest of the people
in my beginner's class are all better
than me. Maybe my center of gravity is off.

The poles attached to my wrists
with Velcro bands are doing no good
at all. I have fallen so many times
I'm sure my butt is one big bruise.
At this rate, I will never get off
the bunny hill. Matt, of course,
has already taken the lift up
to the beginner's slope, which you're
not supposed to do before a full day

on the bunny hill, but Matt is Matt,
and he can do any sport. Dad had told him
not to leave me alone, but he did
anyway.

Meanwhile, we've barely seen
our parents. I personally think
they're hiding out in their room
doing god only knows what,
but I don't want to think
about it too much. I feel very sporty
in my ski attire, even though it's too warm
out for all the layers I have on.

By lunchtime muscles ache
that I didn't even know I had.
I head to the ski lodge to meet
Matt for lunch. I'm trying to take
my last ski off when I slip and fall,
hard, against the whole rack of skis
leaning up against the wall of the lodge.
I can't straighten my back without
a sharp pain coursing through it.

Matt appears at that minute and looks horrified.
He rushes me off to the first aid unit,
even though I assure him I'm not bleeding or broken.
The first aid guy gives me a heating pad
and an ice pack and tells me to alternate
using them for the rest of the day. He suggests

not skiing again for a few days, but we're only here
for three days as it is, so I guess I won't be skiing
   anymore.

Matt insists on coming back to the room
with me and he gets me settled in bed
with the heating pad. "I'll be right back,"
he says, and returns ten minutes later
with a whole bag of candy and magazines
from the gift shop. He sits down on the bed
next to me and says, "What do you want to watch?"
He hands me the remote. I stare at it.
In all of my sixteen years, Matt has never,
ever, given me the remote. Never
underestimate the power of guilt.

I flick around the channels and Matt says,
"Wait, stop there. It's *The Princess Bride.*
Have you seen it?"
I shake my head.

"It's a classic! Last year
it was the big movie in my dorm.
I can quote all the lines from it."

"Please don't," I say. "Let's just watch it."

By the time Inigo has found
the six-fingered man and says,
"My name is Inigo Montoya.

You killed my father. Prepare to die,"
and the six-fingered man says,
"Stop saying that!" I decide
this is a perfect movie, a movie all others
should be compared to, and it occurs to me
that this is the first time Matt and I
have hung out together in years.

Even though my back hurts
and we're stuck inside while the mountain
lies waiting outside our window,
I'm having a really good time eating candy
and laughing with my brother.

When the movie's over, I convince him
to go back out and ski some more.
"Have fun storming the castle," I say
as he leaves.

When I'm alone, I decide to take a bath,
which I figure is like one big heating pad.
I pick up the little shampoo and conditioner bottles
that the hotel provides and bring them in with me.
I'm reminded of being four or five, and staying
in a hotel with my grandparents and slipping
the little bottles into my bag when we left.

For days I was wracked with guilt
and I finally told my mom I had stolen them.
She laughed and said they were free.

That might actually have been the last time
I felt truly guilty about anything.
My moral compass has broken
since then.

As I get in the water and my back twinges,
I think of Princess Buttercup and Westley
from the movie. They had true love,
and it brought him back from the dead.

I lie in the tub and wonder what kind of miracle
it would take to transform me
into the kind of girl
that boys come back from the dead for.

Bloomingdale's

I.

Eliza has started dating
this guy named Nathan
who everyone calls Nate.
(Otherwise you'd have to admit
to having a friend named Nathan,
and that's almost as bad
as a friend named Norman
or Martin or Stewart
or some other name
that is really a grandparent name.)

Nate goes to Blair Academy,
which is just as snooty as it sounds,
but the guys there are all really cute,
or so says Eliza, and she had her pick
of them. She's bringing Nate
to our junior prom, and she said
he has friends who will go with me
and Stefanie, if we want.

I admit, I've wanted to go
to a prom since I got
Prom Barbie in kindergarten.
She looked so happy,
in her pale blue gown,
her silver open-toed shoes,
her glam clutch purse,
and rhinestone diamond earrings.
And Ken in his tux?
Don't even get me started.
A pint-size hottie.

If one of Nate's friends
wants to be the Ken to my Barbie,
that is fine by me. No one
in my own school has asked me,
and the prom is only a month away.

I was kind of hoping Ben Silver
would ask, even though
I've barely spoken to him

since our kiss in eighth grade.
He's not so punk anymore,
more skater-boy who shops
at PacSun. Anyway, it's too late
because Hailey Briggs, my arch-
enemy from elementary school, asked him
and he said yes, so now Hailey is going
to the prom with MY prom date.

Part of me wonders
if Eliza is doing this out of pity
because we don't have dates
and maybe she feels a little sorry
for the things she said to me
on my birthday,
but another part of me
doesn't care and is just happy
she thought of me.

"Can I meet the guy first?"
I ask Eliza. "How will I know
if I like him?"

It turns out the guys want to meet us too,
so we agree on Sbarro's in the food court.
I'm glad, because it's my home turf.

We have an hour before the guys arrive,
so we decide to try on prom dresses

at Bloomingdale's, because Eliza says
that's where everyone gets them.

First we try on all the ones we would
never wear, just for the fun of it.
Stef chooses one with a huge purple bow
across her butt that she says makes her look
like an elephant instead of her usual hippo self,
and Eliza says she shouldn't put herself down
all the time and that she has lost a lot of weight,
which is true, and even though I want to believe
it's because of Weight Watchers,
I kind of wish I had said something that night
at my sleepover, just in case it isn't.

Stef wiggles her butt so the purple bow
dances, and I am glad she seems so happy.
I quickly slip a leopard-print dress over my head
that is so tight it takes both of them to zip it up.
Eliza twirls around in a dress with a hoop in the bottom
of the skirt like a Southern belle would wear
a hundred years ago.

We look at ourselves in the mirror and
laugh until we cry. Eliza snaps a picture
on her camera phone and promises not to load it
on the Internet as blackmail someday.

Then Stef pulls one out from the pile
and hands it to me. "You should try this one.

It will bring out your eyes."
The dress is a pale blue and feels like real silk,
and the second I slip it over my head, I know
it must be mine.
It makes every curve look bigger
and every bulge look smaller.
It makes my eyes and hair shine.
It's a miracle dress!

"Wow," Stefanie and Eliza say in unison.
"How much is it?" Stefanie asks.
"I should have looked before I gave it to you."

"I'm afraid to look.
You do it."

So Stefanie reaches behind me
and pulls the tag out from behind my hair.

"Uh-oh," she says.
"You might want to take it off
really, really carefully in case
they've got one of those 'you break it,
you bought it' policies."

"That bad, huh?"

"Worse," she says.

"Well, it doesn't matter
what it costs," Eliza declares.
"You HAVE to get this dress."

I gaze at my reflection again.
I can count on one hand the number
of times that I've looked
in the mirror and been pleased
at who looked back.

I shake my head and begin
unzipping it very carefully.
"It would pretty much wipe
out my savings account."
A few years ago I realized
that if I decide not to go to college,
my parents will probably cut me off,
and I better have some money
of my own. I have enough
to last me a few months.

If my parents had let me work
in one of the zillions of mall stores
that are always looking for help, I wouldn't
have to worry, but no, they said that being
a teenager is a full-time job,
whatever that means.
So the only money I have is the result
of trying to save a portion of each allowance

and all of the birthday checks
from my grandparents.
It's a good thing I don't have much
of a social life, so I don't have a lot
to spend money on.

I'm almost out of the dress
when a saleswoman comes in
and says, "When you're done
with that, honey, can you pass it
here? I have a request
for it from another store.
Seems like your size
is a hot commodity this year."
What would Prom Barbie do?
Beautiful dress that makes me
feel like a princess,
or financial independence?

Oh, who am I kidding, this is Barbie!
"I'm going to take it," I blurt out.

When the lady leaves,
Stefanie says, "Are you crazy?
You could buy a used CAR
for the cost of that dress!"

I clutch the dress tighter.
"Must have dress. Must have dress."

Eliza stands between me
and Stefanie. "Leave her alone.
You just don't understand fashion."

Stefanie sighs. "Well, you better decide fast,
because we're gonna be late,
and I don't think that's the best impression."

I turn to Eliza. "I don't have enough
cash on me."

Eliza lifts the dress out of my arms.
"You can pay me back tomorrow,"
she says, and marches out of the dressing room
before I can change my mind.

II.

My dress bag rests solidly, happily, on my lap
as we wait for the guys. Every boy that walks by
who looks like he could be in high school
I imagine is him.

So far he's been tall and skinny,
short and fat, short and skinny,
and once he was even bald
with a nose ring.
Eliza has never met him,
so she's no help.

The good part is that we were able
to scarf down pizza without them
watching, so now when they come
we can daintily pick at a salad.

When they finally do show up,
they are really cute in a "private school
boy" kind of way
with the blazers and everything.

I'm pleased, and I can tell Stefanie
is too because she pushes her hair
out of her eyes.

I'm paired up with Jake,
who is a little taller than me,
with gray eyes and black hair.
The collar of his shirt is popped,
a trend from the eighties that should have stayed
in the eighties if you ask me.
"I've never seen anyone with gray eyes
before," I tell him as we get in line
for our food. I figure this is better
than telling him his shirt makes him look
like a preppy vampire.

"Colored contacts," he says.

"Oh," I say. "Cool."

And that's pretty much the high point
of our conversation. Jake isn't a big talker,
but he seems sweet. He buys my salad for me.

We decide we're going to do the prom up right:
corsages, pictures with fawning parents,
limo, Champagne, the whole shebang.
I even show him a corner of my dress
because he says he wants to get a bowtie
and cummerbund to match. I don't know
what a cummerbund is, but as long as he does,
I won't worry about it.

Meanwhile Stefanie is really hitting it off
with her guy, and Eliza and Nate
haven't taken their hands or lips
off each other since Nate arrived.

When I get home and try on my dress
for my parents, Dad says, "You'll be
the belle of the ball." Mom actually gets weepy.
"Whatever you paid, I'll cover it,"
she says, wiping a tear from her eye.

Woo-hoo!

III.

The day of the prom, Mom brings me
to the fanciest salon in the mall
and I get a manicure, pedicure,
and a hot-oil treatment for my hair.
I actually enjoy being with her,
who for the first time in my memory
doesn't say one single negative thing.

The fairy tale has begun!

Stefanie, Eliza, and their parents come
to my house, and the guys pull up
in the limo. It's like a scene from a movie –
a beautiful day, girls in long gowns,
cute guys in tuxes, sappy parents.

It's all exactly like I imagined.
And that's the problem.
I feel like I'm going through the motions
of a girl going to the prom.
I'm all made up, my hair's done,
my dress is perfect, my strappy sandals
are new and stiff, the limo is rockin',
the Champagne is flowing, and the boys
are already drunk by the time we get to the hotel.
The guy taking the official pictures
is bald except for a long ponytail,
the cocktail hour has tiny hot dogs,

the chaperones keep yelling at everyone
to stop grinding on the dance floor,
the punch is spiked, the chicken is rubbery,
two girls are fighting in the bathroom
while another barfs into the sink, four kids
get kicked out for lighting up a joint,
a girl is crying because her date hooked up
with her now ex-best friend right in front of her,
another girl's dress rips,
and one of the teachers who came prepared
for such emergencies has to sew it up.
It's all so predictable
I want to cry.

When the prom is half over,
Jake mentions the hotel room.
I shouldn't even be surprised, but I am.

"What hotel room?"

"Didn't Eliza tell you?"

I shake my head.

"We're all staying over tonight."

Now, I may be a little drunk from the punch,
but I'd remember if I was supposed to pack
a bag and lie to my parents.

Those aren't the kinds of details
I'd be likely to forget.

When I point out our lack of bags,
he says, "We've got all we need right here,"
and pulls me closer.

Something inside me snaps.
It's not that Jake is a bad person.
He's a totally normal horny teenage boy
and everyone knows
what prom night is famous for.
It just occurs to me
that I don't feel anything for him,
and I don't want to be here anymore.

So I tell him I'll be right back,
but I don't really intend to be.
I don't want my friends to see me
leave, or they might come after me,
and I really want to be alone.

I try to sneak out the door behind
the DJ, but suddenly I fly over
a thick cord and wind up flat on my back,
looking up at the big strobe light.
The music has stopped. Darn these heels!
Darn the punch that I drank too much of,
even though I knew it was spiked.
So much for a quick exit.

I don't wait to find out if anyone saw me,
I just run from the room.
I totally have to go to the bathroom
but there's no way I can risk it now,
and then I remember the hotel room.
I give the lady at the front desk
Nate's name, and she hands me a key,
no questions asked.

As I'm waiting impatiently for the elevator,
I hear two guys talking behind me.
"Yeah, some girl tripped on it,
and that cord is shredded, man.
No more music tonight."

"No way."

"Way."

"Insane."

"Totally."

"Do you know who it was?"

The elevator finally arrives
before I can hear the answer
and I throw myself in it.
Unfortunately, I throw myself
directly on Hailey Briggs and Ben Silver,

along with Rick Vinik and his date,
Hailey's friend Jessica, who hates
me almost as much as Hailey does.

"Watch it!" Hailey says, pushing me off
of her before breezing out the door.
The others follow. Then Ben turns back, and sticks
his foot into the doorway so the elevator door
doesn't close. "Are you okay?" he asks.

And it occurs to me – I am just like the girl
in all those movies who is a loser
until she becomes beautiful for the prom,
which she thought would be the highlight
of her life, but when she realizes it isn't,
she walks off, head held high. If I'm that girl,
then why can't I walk off gracefully?
Why do I have to trip over cords
and plow into these four, of all people?

Ben asks again if I'm okay, but all
I see are his lips moving and remember how they felt
on mine, even though it was four years ago
and he probably doesn't even remember our silly game.

And then I think, what would Prom Barbie do now,
or the girl in the movie,
and I have no idea what that would be,
but I know what I have to do.

I step forward and kiss Ben right on the lips.
Then I press the button for our floor
and wait for the doors to close dramatically.

But they don't close because Ben's foot
is still in the way.

I meet his gaze. His eyes are very wide.
He doesn't look mad, though. But Hailey does,
storming up behind him. Rick, who saw
the whole thing, laughs.

So I do the only thing I can. I push Ben backwards
so his foot clears the path of the door.
And then I call out to Rick,
"I stole your egg in fourth grade,"
and the doors finally close,
and just as dramatically as I'd hoped.

IV.

By the time I get to the room
I no longer have to use the bathroom
so I sit down on one of the beds
and wonder what to do next.
Does anyone even know
I'm missing yet?

I turn on the television and find myself
right in the middle of my favorite
Princess Bride scene. I'm just in time
to hear Miracle Max say, "Have fun
storming the castle," and I know
I've made the right choice
in leaving the party.

A few minutes later, I hear voices
in the hall and I freeze.
Through the door I hear:

"She must be in here," Jake says.
"The television is on."

They knock and call my name
but I don't answer.
They must not have stopped for a key.

"Leave it to Tessa," Eliza says,
"to create all this drama."

Gee, thanks, Eliza!

"She just doesn't know
how to express herself," Stefanie says,
sounding tipsy. "So she never takes,
what do you call it?" she slurs.
"*Responsibility* for her, you know,
actions. It's classic Tessa."

Not true!
Is it?

"Not to mention she just made
your prom the quietest prom
in history," Nate adds.

Okay, so I guess they do know
it was me who ripped the cord.

I tiptoe into the bathroom.
The tub is huge so I pull back
the shower curtain and lie down,
cringing as my dress splits
right up the back.

I can't believe Eliza said that
about me creating drama.
I don't do that, do I? From now on,
I plan on blending into the woodwork.
No one will notice me.
I'll wear all black, never raise
my hand in class, never flirt again.
Only one more year of high school left.
Mom was right after all. Being a teenager
is a full-time job.

But still, I'd like to think
my friends would be a little more
supportive.

After all, if they thought about
it, they would see the truth.

II.

It's not *my* fault
there's nothing magical
about this fairy tale.

Lost, and Found Again

I wake up to Jake tapping me
on the shoulder. "Are you ready
to go home?"

Darn that lady at the front desk
being so free with the room keys!
I am about to tell him to bugger off
when it suddenly occurs to me
that instead of the cold tile
of the hotel bathtub,
I'm lying on something soft.
My eyes spring open.
The first thing I see
is a row of lockers.
The next thing I see

is Nail Boy standing over me,
grinning in that Cheshire Cat
way of his. He is the one asking
me if I want to go home, not Jake.

I can't process what's going on.
My head is still filled
with all those things I did.
All those emotions I felt,
or worse yet, the ones I *hadn't* felt.

Am I ready to go home?
My brain tells me
I'm in the Lost and Found Office
at the mall, and wasn't the mall
the place I once called home?
But after everything I've been through,
I'm not so sure anymore.
I rub my eyes and sit up.
Normally this is where
I would say something sarcastic or beg him
to tell me what's going on, but I don't
have the energy.

I am spent.

Nail Boy smiles and holds out his hand.
"Come. We don't have much time."
He takes my arm and helps me up
from the old couch.

He hands me my gym key and says,
"I put your bag back in the locker.
I don't think you'll be needing it anymore."

I'm still groggy and confused
as I stumble behind him.
It feels like years since he left me
holding that baby shoe. And what about pulling
the plug on me? What was that about?

I try to muster up the strength to ask,
but he is moving so quickly
it's all I can do to keep up.
We pass the fountain, and for the first time
in my life, I don't have the urge
to steal someone's wish.

He hurries past the tree of life,
past the twelve-plex and the DDR machine,
past the Dippin' Dots, which would taste
very refreshing right now,
past the carousel, which is stuck as usual,
past the bungee trampolines and the sandbox,
and right up to the smooth wooden door
marked "Chapel – nondenominational."

I haven't been here since I was twelve
and Old Bev and Old Abe
renewed their wedding vows after
they found out the minister who married

them fifty years ago was really just a guy
who sold pickles and who'd rented
a minister's outfit from a costume shop.
I never thought I'd have a reason
to step foot in it again.

"Hurry," he says as I stop outside the door
to watch a little girl throw handfuls of sand
gleefully into the air. She looks so free.
Without a care in the world. I want that.
I want that more than I've ever wanted
anything.

He ducks inside the small doorway
and pulls me in after him.
I follow him to the front pew,
my feet dragging. My stomach hurts,
and I've never felt so weak.

Nail Boy helps me sit and says,
"Do you understand why
you had to take your journey?
Did you remember the question
you had asked yourself,
back in the gym?"

It takes effort to raise my head,
but I force myself to meet
his eyes. And I realize I always knew.

I knew the question,
and I knew the answer.

My voice catches in my throat
and when it comes out, it comes
out small. "I had asked myself
why I didn't duck
when the ball came at me."

"Why didn't you duck?" he asks,
"when the ball came at you?"

My eyes look past his face.
"I didn't duck," I tell him,
"because I believed
I had it coming to me."

"Why?" he repeats.

I feel even fainter now, like I'm half asleep.
I force myself to answer. To get this over with.
"Because basically I'm a bad person.
Good people don't lie and cheat
and steal. Everyone knows that.
Even I know that.
Someone forgot
to teach me
there are consequences
for my actions,
even if I never get caught."

He smiles. "You even blame someone else
for not teaching you about consequences."

I give a small smile back. "See what I mean?
I'm hopeless." My eyes fill with tears,
which they almost never do.

Nail Boy doesn't say anything.
I mean, what is there to say?
I wonder if I can lie down
on this bench? It suddenly feels
very inviting. If I could just curl
up here, I think everything would
be okay. If I could just shut my eyes,
just for a minute even, I can pretend
that my old fountain wish came true
and all those memories were someone
else's memories, someone I maybe passed
in the hall one day. That way
I wouldn't have to feel the way
I do right now, which is that I wish
I had done a lot of things
differently.

But they weren't someone else's.
It's time I owned them. They weren't
all bad, I suppose. There were times
I felt hopeful and happy and content.
And there were memories not found
in that bag where I laughed and sang

and felt like a semi-normal person,
but I guess those weren't the ones
I needed to see.

But a lot of the time
I felt anxious and angry
and alone and lost
and the walls I built around
myself just got thicker and thicker.

Nail Boy breaks in. "What else
did those memories tell you?"

I shake my head.

"What else?" he repeats,
more forcefully this time.

"Nothing!" I reply.

"WHAT ELSE?" he booms.
The fake stained glass in the chapel
shakes and shivers
and the cobwebs in my brain clear
a bit.

"That I'm strong!"
I am practically yelling
and it feels good.

"That I'm resourceful!
That I've made a lot of bad choices
and some good ones, too.
But somehow along the way,
I forgot to figure out who I was,
who I wanted to be.
Is that what you're looking for?"

Instead of answering me,
a faint redness creeps into his cheeks.
Almost shyly, he asks, "Tessa,
don't you know you sparkle?"

I am now fully awake. "I *sparkle*?"
I would laugh if I could.

"I bet if you go through the rest
of your life telling yourself,
'I'm sparkling,'
you'll have a whole different energy
and experience."

I chuckle. "If I *have* a rest of my life, that is."

He leans forward and locks
his eyes with mine.
"I'm going to tell you a secret.
Our lives are shaped by the future,
not by the past. Once you decide
how you want your life to be,

all you need to do
is live into that future."

Then quietly he asks,
"If you have a rest of your life,
what are you going to do differently?"
He reaches out to touch my hand
and when he does,
it's like a jolt of electricity
passes between us. I look up,
and into his eyes, and I think,
I'm sparkling. I sparkle.

And then I answer.
"The next time a dodgeball
is fired at my head,
I'm going to catch it."

He takes my hand and we sit there
like that for a few minutes. The lights flicker
in the chapel. I know it's time.
I close my eyes.

County General

Ah, gotta love the smell
of disinfectant and pee.
I open my eyes and try
not to inhale too deeply.
My mom runs out
to get the doctor, and Matt
looks at me and starts crying.
I haven't seen him cry
since he was ten
and he learned that even a fake sword
can hurt if you plunge it
into your foot.

I tentatively turn my head
to the side, and am glad

to discover the brace is gone.
I rub my neck. It feels much better.
I thought Nail Boy's hand
would still be in mine.
But it's not.

"Where's Nail Boy, I mean,
the guy with a long nail thingy
stuck in his head?"

Matt wipes his nose
with the back of his jacket and says,
"Boy, they must have given you
some good painkillers."

"What do you mean?"

"Just that I have no idea
who you're talking about."

"But he told me he met you.
He said you were cool."

"Um, Tessa? Don't you think
I'd remember if I met a guy
with a nail sticking out of his head?"

I sigh in defeat.
"Pinch me," I tell Matt.

"Huh?"

"Pinch me," I command,
holding out my arm.
I need to know what's real
and what isn't.

He pinches me.

"Ow!" I rub my arm.

"You said to pinch you!"

"You didn't have to do it so hard.
Well, at least I know I'm really here."

His brows scrunch up. "Where else
would you be?"

"Could be anywhere," I tell him.
"Could be the mall. Could be the prom.
Could even be snooping under your mattress."

"You're not making any sense, Tess."
He blows his nose loudly.
"Try not to fall into any more comas.
It was pretty scary.
Mom and Dad were totally freaked.
I told her not to dress you in that."

I lift up the blanket and peer underneath.
I am wearing a pink sundress,
the likes of which I have not seen
since I was six and still allowing Mom
to dress me. But it's actually not so bad.

My parents run in along with a doctor,
who pronounces me healed and says
I can go home in a day or two,
but I'll have to stay in bed for another week.

My parents beam down at me
and I look at them, really look at them,
and try to rid myself of any preconceived
idea of who they are. They look older
and smaller and when they hug me
and kiss my cheeks, I know they mean it,
and I feel my heart get bigger
like the way the Grinch's does in
that TV special, and I wonder
if Nail Boy really *was* the Ghost of Christmas Past
even though he said he wasn't.

When Mom tells me the first thing
she's going to do when I'm well enough
is to take me for a facial because this hospital
air will dry out anyone's skin,
I just smile and say okay,
but only if she'll come with me.

Because I know that by trying to fix me,
she is really trying to fix herself.

Dad says I can wear anything
I want to school and he promises
not to make me change. But then he says,
"Never mind. I can't promise
that! How about I just take you for an ice cream?"
I see Mom stiffen beside him
at the mention of feeding me ice cream
but for once she doesn't say anything.

And I realize
that my dad might not be the greatest
dad of all time,
I mean, he's a little temperamental
and works too much,
but he never stopped
trying to protect me
and trying to make me feel special.
I just stopped listening.

My mom tells me they are going
to leave to get some sleep and I wonder
if that means they haven't slept
the whole time I was here,
but I'm feeling too overwhelmed
by everything to ask.

They kiss me goodbye,
which now doubles the amount
of times they've kissed me in a year,
and Matt says he'll follow
in a few minutes.

"I just wanted to tell you," he says,
fiddling with the zipper on his jacket,
"that I'm really glad you're okay."

I smile and am about to thank him
for coming home from college
when lo and behold, Nail Boy comes
into the room! Except his head is wrapped
in white bandages. No more nail.
My heart pounds.

Nail Boy gives Matt a wave,
and Matt says hey, and they do this total guy thing
where they touch knuckles.

"I thought you didn't know him,"
I say to Matt reproachfully.

"Oh, you meant *this* guy?"
Matt asks innocently.
"You said a guy with a nail
sticking out of his head.
I don't see any nail."

"Drill bit," Nail Boy and I say in unison.
Then we laugh. Matt leaves us,
and I pat the bedside next to me.
"You have a lot of explaining to do, mister."

He sits down, but he doesn't take my hand.
He looks a bit worried. "I'm sorry," he says.
"About pulling the plug on you.
I was just kidding around. That machine
wasn't even hooked up to anything.
But then you had this look of fear
on your face, and then you slipped
back into the coma and I felt really, really bad."

I stare at him. "That plug wasn't hooked up?
Then why did I wind up back at the mall?"

He shrugs. "Maybe you weren't done yet."

"I guess I wasn't," I say.

Neither of us speaks for a minute.
Then he asks, "Are you done now?"

I consider this. "I'm not sure.
I think it's going to take a while."

He reaches his hand toward mine,
and I watch intently as it comes
ever closer. Then . . . electricity.

We sit there like that, not speaking,
all my focus on our hands lying there
until the nurse comes in with a tray
and tells him I need to eat and rest
and that he can come back later.
As he ducks out of the room,
he turns back to me and winks.

My eyes open wide. "Wait!" I call out
after him, but he doesn't come back.

The nurse says, "How do you two know
each other? You just woke up
a little while ago."

"You wouldn't believe me
if I told you," I say, flopping back
onto the pillow.

"If you say so," she says, putting
down the tray. There is a card on top
of it, which I reach for.
It's from Stefanie and Eliza.
"Nothing is the same without you."

And just like that, I forget what they said
at the prom and I promise myself
I'm going to be a much better friend
because, honestly, I thought everything
would be exactly the same without me.

As I slurp the split-pea soup,
which actually is pretty tasty,
I decide that when I get home,
I'm going to write down
the best parts of my childhood.
They weren't the times I was vengeful
or sneaky or mean
or suspicious or hurting.

The best times were
when I felt sparkling,
like trying on the makeup with Eliza,
and swimming in the pond with Naomi
and eating the Snickers on the roof
and visiting the three-legged cat
and kissing Ben
and running through the woods at camp
and bouncing on the mall trampoline
and watching *The Princess Bride* with Matt
and shopping for prom dresses with Eliza and Stef
and touching Nail Boy's hand the first time, even if it
   wasn't real
(or was it?)
because those are the times
that I felt like I knew
who I was.
Those are the times
when the walls were down.
And I can't see
through walls.

READER'S GUIDE

1. How would you describe Tessa? Is she a likable character? Does she seem a bit misguided? How would you depict her family life? Would you call it healthy? Why or why not?

2. After not being able to select her preferred Halloween costume, Tessa remarks, "I think Miss Rudder was wrong. I don't think you can be anything you want to be." (p. 58) Tessa clearly is not just talking about the elf costume, so what else does she mean by that statement?

3. After realizing that she left her teddy bear in her grandmother's car, Tessa continues to pretend Teddy is missing. Why do you think she did this?

4. Tessa remembers the time when she was four or five and "stole" the little bottles of shampoo from a hotel. She was wracked with guilt. "That might actually have been the last time I felt truly guilty about anything. My moral compass has broken since then." (p. 214) Explain Tessa's comment. Cite various examples from the book of how her moral compass has broken.

5. Describe the relationship between Tessa and her friends. Who are her friends? Do you think Tessa is able to be a good friend? Why or why not?

6. If you were Tessa, what kind of person would you be? Does Tessa have a positive or negative sense of self?

7. All in all, do you think that Tessa feels badly about the things she has done? What has Tessa learned from her near-death experience? Do you think she'll become a better person?